I0716100

A CHRISTMAS *Wedding*

A Novella

—SMALL TOWN CHRISTMAS—
BOOK 6

D. ALLEN

A Christmas Wedding
Small Town Christmas, Book 6
Copyright © 2021 by D. Allen
Batavia, NY

www.DavidNethBooks.com

ISBN: 978-1-945336-21-8
First Edition

Subscribe to the author's newsletter for updates and exclusive content:
DavidNethBooks.com/Newsletter

Follow the author at:
www.facebook.com/DavidNethBooks
www.instagram.com/DavidNethBooks

ALSO BY D. ALLEN

MONTANA BEACH
SUMMER STAY

SUMMER JOB

SUMMER NIGHTS

SMALL TOWN CHRISTMAS
A CHRISTMAS REUNION

A CHRISTMAS CHARADE

A CHRISTMAS SPARK

A CHRISTMAS SONG

A CHRISTMAS DEPARTURE

A CHRISTMAS WEDDING

STANDALONE
SNOW AFTER CHRISTMAS

December 3rd
Lexi

❄ ❄ ❄

The first Friday of the month is possibly the worst time to be working at a bank. Between the regular Friday afternoon rush with cashing checks, deposits, and withdrawals, there's also the fact that it's the beginning of the Christmas season. Savings bonds, savings accounts, loan applications, or those people who request a *crisp* fifty dollar bill to put in their Christmas cards.

The lobby is packed with people, many of whom are too impatient to wait in line so they're grumpy by time they get up to me. I feel bad for Bob Luther, the maintenance guy who is trying to put up the lobby Christmas tree in the midst of all of this madness.

"Five more minutes, Lex, and then Rachel's going to

be replacing you," Carol, the evening manager, tells me as she passes behind my teller line.

Hallelujah.

After being on my feet all day—and forcing myself to be pleasant through more than one verbal attack on my competence—all I want to do is go home and relax in the tub with a good book and some Christmas music playing softly throughout my apartment.

I'm a little weird in that I like to put on instrumental Christmas music, light a sugar cookie-scented candle, and slip into a warm bubble bath all while reading books about crazed psycho-killers. If it wasn't completely unsanitary to eat in the bathroom, I'd probably be enjoying a nice gingerbread cookie as well. I haven't been able to bring myself to cross that line of weird yet.

Almost robotically, I count out the bills for the customer and slide her receipt across the counter to her. As my hand moves, the glint of my engagement ring reminds me that after work I need to rush over to LeRoy, the next town over, to meet up with my fiancé, Walt, and his family to finalize yet more wedding plans. For a wedding that's only twenty-one days away, there is still a lot left to do.

Getting married on Christmas Eve sounded so romantic when it was first suggested. Now I'm kicking myself for going with the idea. How do I prepare for *the* biggest day of my life while also trying to enjoy the Christmas season? Christmas time has always been my favorite season, but this year it just seems like it's all passing by so fast. How is it already December?

Next up is a nervous old man with a zipped packet filled with cash. "I'd like to make a deposit," he says to me. "And a withdrawal."

"Put up your closed sign," Carol tells me from behind. "After this gentleman, count your drawer and then you're free to go."

Happily, I set my "See Next Teller" sign just above my work station, facing out to the customers. Smiling at the old man, I ask him if he's filled out a despot slip yet.

Of course he hasn't. And he would like to know the balances on all of his accounts, which will determine how much he wants to take *out*.

Five minutes turns into ten, then fifteen. Rachel takes her spot in the teller line beside mine, already beginning her shift. I watch the clock as I finish helping the old man, who wishes me a "Merry Christmas" that helps relieve the growing resentment I'd been building toward him.

After counting down my drawer and waiting for Carol to count it down too, I grab my things from the break room — Walt's left me two voicemails — and hurry out to my car.

Even though I only live around the corner, it was a good thing I drove here this morning. Walt's parents are waiting for me and it'll take at least twenty minutes to get there, longer by time I park and meet them inside. And if there's one thing I learned about Walt's family, it's that you don't keep them waiting. Luckily, my tardiness due to my respectable job at a bank will soften the blow. But only a little.

On the ride over, I sing along to Mariah Carey's "All I Want for Christmas Is You," stopping before she goes into the really high notes so I don't embarrass myself. Alone in the car is my moment to unwind a little before I need to act like the perfect fiancée in front of Prudence and Walter the Second. At least *my* Walter (the Third) isn't as high strung.

Being outside makes me a little depressed, though. This year has been unseasonably warm and the lack of snow makes it seem like we're just going through the motions for Christmas and not that it's actually here. Supposedly there's a chance of snow by Christmas, but so far I don't have my hopes up.

By time I pull into the long driveway leading into the gorgeous event center that will serve as the venue for our wedding, I'm nearly half an hour late.

Rushing to the front door, I let myself inside and step into the grand foyer. With oak panels and hardwood floors, the whole atmosphere is regal elegance, matched by the crystal chandelier hanging above the entrance. To the left is a reception room and to the right is the formal dining room, where I hear familiar voices.

"Lexi, you made it," Walt says with a smile. He steps toward me and offers a polite kiss to the cheek. Dressed in a navy blue suit and shiny brown leather shoes, he is very much in his Walter the Third frame of mind. All about appearances. Being that he's ten years older than me, I always feel like he has so much to teach me about how to be proper.

Until I learn everything he knows, I do my best not to look like trash that he decided to drag home. He says I'm always too hard on myself, but there must be a reason for my insecurities around his family, right?

"Alexis, dear, there you are," Prudence says in her monotone voice. "We didn't think you would make it." She steps toward me to offer a brief, limp hug. She has on a blue skirt with a deep neckline, where a diamond sits squarely between her breasts.

Walter the Second, dressed much like his son but in a gray suit and black shoes, nods at me with a tight-lipped smile. "Good evening."

I take off my coat and fold it over my arm. "Sorry I'm late. I got caught up at work."

"Mr. Woodward will take that for you," Prudence says.

The other man standing in the room steps toward me and takes my coat.

"Thank you," I offer.

"We were just discussing how we wanted the

room set up," Walt tells me.

"Oh, so this is where the wedding will take place?" I ask. Last I knew, the ceremony would be in the library by the fireplace. To me, that felt cozy and the pictures we were shown about how it was decorated for Christmas gave me a warm and fuzzy feeling.

And now, apparently, that had changed.

"Yes, we thought this would offer more room for all of your guests." Prudence surveys the room with a thoughtful hand on her chin.

All of the guests who I will probably meet for the first time at my wedding. How delightful.

"I think down in front of the window would look stunning, don't you think?" she goes on.

"We've had many couples choose that location to exchange vows," Mr. Woodward says. "With the backdrop of the yard and landscaping, it could be very beautiful. Even if it does snow, it adds a certain contrast to the room."

"I don't think we'll be getting any snow this year," Walter says with a chuckle.

"I hope we do," Walt says. "It'll look nice for the wedding."

"Oh, but think of the guests," Walter counters. "They wouldn't want to trample in the weather like that. And then it's tracking inside."

I sit quietly and simply follow the conversation as each person speaks.

"Yes, well, we cannot control the weather, can we?" Prudence says. "Let's discuss what we can control. What do you think about the set up Mr. Woodward suggested, sweetheart?"

Everyone in the room knows she's talking to Walt. At least one of us gets a say.

Realizing that my arrival hasn't changed the wedding plans much, I take in the beauty of the room. Tray ceilings with soft, bright lighting, giving the whole room a sense of timeless grace. Not a speck of dust is in the room.

That's when I notice my feet are aching from standing in my heels all day. What I wouldn't give to take them off and soak my feet. Better yet, I would love to have a job where I didn't have to wear heels all the time.

If I actually built up the courage to open my own bakery and start my own business, I could go to work in sneakers, or the controversial crocs, and feel more accomplished with my day. Sure, I might be making less than I am now, but every dollar I earned would be from my own hard work. It would mean so much more.

Plus, I would enjoy it. All the creations I could come up with. Cakes, breads, pies... You name it, I'd bake it. I've already been told by several people that my scones are —

"Alexis, are you listening?" Prudence asks me.

"Huh? I'm sorry?" I blink and realize everyone is

staring at me.

"I asked," she starts with a hint of annoyance, "which you think would be better: setting the desserts on a separate table away from the entrées or having them brought out later after dinner has been served?"

"Um…well…" I look around the room and motion to one end. "The entrées will be set out over here?"

"That is one of the options," Mr. Woodward says. "Or we could set them up in the reception hall, however, those would need to be removed before be began playing music."

Lexi didn't envision a lively dance session, but she was going to give Walter and Prudence the benefit of the doubt. Maybe they'd let Walt off his leash for one night. Or they'd be too distracted to see him be himself. It was always interesting to me how Walt seems to have a different persona for whoever he was alone with.

"Personally, I think setting out the dessert ahead of time might be a mistake," Prudence declared. "What would be stopping people from taking a dessert with their entrée? And if everyone has already had dessert, who would pay attention when it's time to cut the cake? That's a precious photo opportunity."

Wouldn't want to miss that.

"Alexis is the baker," Walter the Second says.

"Let's have her decide."

Suddenly, there are four sets of eyes on me and my stammering only worsens. "Well, I…uh…I'll have to—"

Walt steps toward me and hooks his arm around my waist. "She's an artist. She'll need time to think."

"Right," I say with a nod.

"But we have to make a decision," Prudence insists.

"And we will," Walt says. "But we also want it done right."

She nods slowly, conceding to his logic. "Well, if we are done discussing the food, perhaps we should look at setups for photos. Mr. Woodward, can you show us some of the more popular places to take photos?"

"Certainly! Follow me."

As Mr. Woodward leads them out of the room, I hold Walt back.

"Thanks for saving me," I tell him. "I kind of zoned out there for a while."

"It's okay," he says.

His hands start at my waist, move to my back, then my arms, before sliding down and holding my hands in his. Every touch with his is a bit awkward, almost premeditated.

"I'm sorry for my parents kind of taking over the wedding," he adds. "But since they're paying for it, I kind of couldn't object."

I sigh and look around the room. "It will certainly be beautiful." Almost like a magazine. Staged, but still real, to a degree.

His hands move to the sides of my face—again, unable to find a natural spot. "Listen, for the desserts, I'm going to tell my parents that you're completely in charge."

I make a face and groan, pulling his hands away from my face and holding them in mine. "Walt, no. What if I mess it up?"

"It's just dessert! Besides, it's our wedding."

"That *they're* paying for." I clamp my mouth shut. "Sorry, that was rude."

He nods slowly, agreeing without making a big deal of it. "Just do your best. I'll make sure my parents butt out."

"That's what I'm afraid of. Your mother…" I pause, searching for the right way to phrase it. "Your mother doesn't really like surprises."

He rubs my arms, sending chills throughout my body, and not the good kind. After a minute, I've already had enough and grab his hands again to keep them still.

"She'll have to be surprised with this one," he says. "We all will."

My eyes widen. "You're not even going to help?"

He shrugs. "I want to see what you can do on your own. I know you have it in you."

"I'm going to need help," I tell him. "I need to

know what's typical. What kind of manpower will be available that day. The logistics, you know?"

"So I'll talk to Mr. Woodward before I leave tonight and make sure he connects you with someone who can help you with all of that."

I let out a deep breath, still nervous. "Are you sure?"

Walt gives me a quick peck. "Of course. I trust you."

At least one of us has faith in me.

MY STOMACH GRUMBLES by time I pull into a parking spot off of Jackson Street. The closer I get to home, the more layers of my mask that I peel off. My car that is several years old, my apartment above an empty storefront with public parking. Both of these distinct aspects of my life I hide or try to mute when in the presence of Walt or his parents.

As I cross Jackson, I hover before unlocking the door that leads up to my apartment. The storefront downstairs is empty and its one that I've always dreamt of running my bakery out of long before I even moved upstairs. In some twisted way, I thought living in the building would get me closer to my dream. But dreams don't work unless you do and so far, other than baking up a storm all year long in my tiny efficiency kitchen, I haven't done a damn thing to get closer to that dream of running my own bakery. I've seen too many businesses come and go, both at the bank and from just being around town. Operating a small business is too risky. And, unlike Walt, I don't have parents to lean on if I fall flat on my face.

With a heavy sigh and one last look into the empty shop, I unlock the door leading upstairs and escape to my little apartment. Inside, I shed off more layers of my façade: my business attire, my makeup, my posture as I stand and wait for my leftover chicken to heat up in the microwave.

To fill the air, I put on a Christmas music shuffle as I eat my dinner over the sink. When I'm done, I toss the to-go container in the trash and step into the bathroom to run a bath.

I have twenty-one days left of being a bachelorette, and I'm already beginning to miss it.

DECEMBER 4TH
Jeff

❄ ❄ ❄

The sun shining through the window shines on my face and wakes me from my slumber. I reach up above my head and my hand butts into the wall. Stretching my feet out beyond the edge of the mattress results in a kick to a storage tote stacked in the corner.

The life of a single man, living wherever anyone will take him.

Groaning, I roll toward the windowsill and squint as I reach for my phone. It's just before eight o'clock in the morning. Guess that's a reasonable time to get up.

Lurching forward, I toss my feet to the floor in the small space between stacks of storage containers. The path has been cleared solely for the purpose of allowing me access to the bed. Someday, this will be the bedroom of my future niece or nephew. Until they make their arrival, I get to claim a small corner of it for a place to crash every night.

Shuffling out of the tiny spare bedroom, I make my way downstairs and see my brother, Michael, standing at the window looking out onto the street. If it weren't for the Christmas tree standing in the corner and the wreaths on the doors of his neighbors' houses, it would be hard to tell that it's even Christmas time. Everything is still green. Last week the temperature was even pushing sixty degrees before it dropped back into the thirties and forties. Even though we've woken up to a little dusting of snow a few times, there hasn't been any substantial amount and none in sight in the forecast.

"It's all so green," I say.

Michael nods. "Mm-hmm. Not like the winters we used to have."

Back when we were younger, it seemed like we were sledding right after Thanksgiving. One year, we were almost snowed in at Uncle Pete's after Thanksgiving dinner. Guess the change in the weather shows how many years have truly passed since I was a kid. So much has changed.

"Now we get rain for Christmas instead of snow," I say.

"We still have most of the month," he says. "It could change."

"I doubt it."

"There's more coffee in the pot," he says to change the subject.

I know he doesn't like my realism—he calls it pessimism—but there are times I equally get annoyed with how he's always trying to look at the bright side of things. Can't I just take a moment to wallow every once in a while?

Still, I take the hint and step into the kitchen to pour myself a cup of coffee. Michael follows.

"How'd you sleep?"

"As good as can be expected on a twin bed in that confined jail cell you put me in." I take a seat at the small table in the corner.

He smiles. "Hey, it's not like I locked the door. *You* chose to close it."

"Pardon me for wanting some privacy."

"Are you sure you didn't want to keep it open?" He leans against the counter and smiles as he raises his mug to take a sip. "Just in case the bogeyman tries to get you?"

I grin. "Keep it up. I'll find someone else's house to crash."

"Well then, in that case…"

"Hey!" The back-and-forth brings a smile to my face. After everything I've lost, at least this easy relationship with Michael remains. "You know, even though babies are small and everything, they still need a lot of space. At the very least, a decluttered bedroom."

Michael looks out the kitchen door and then shushes me with a stern look. "Shh, not too loud!"

"What?" I whisper.

"Maddie's still upset she didn't get pregnant last month," he says in a soft voice. "We thought she — she really believed it had worked that time."

Michael and his wife have been trying to have a baby for a few months now. Maybe longer. They only told me they were trying because I came home when they were in the middle of an argument about another negative test. Michael was trying to comfort Maddie and, like me, she just wanted to mourn what they didn't have yet. I know my sleeping in the future nursery isn't helping any.

"Oh, sorry," I murmur.

"It's fine. Just don't mention babies around her, okay?"

I nod. "Got it. You two have been trying for a while now. Are you going to see a specialist or something?"

"We're probably going to give it a few more tries still," he says. "I'm thinking after the stress of the holidays and…everything…that she'll take some pressure off of herself and maybe something will happen. Or not."

The "everything" he mentioned is me. The sooner I get out of here, maybe the sooner Maddie will have a bun in the oven. Take the stress off of her and put it on me to find a new place.

"If you want, I can help clean out that room with you before I go to work," I offer. "I could use the extra space and I think you could use the distraction. Maybe if you two start dressing up the nursery, Maddie will get her mind off of *making* a baby."

"Maybe." He doesn't seem to agree with my logic, but he adds, "Yeah, let's clean that room out after lunch. I've been meaning to get to it anyway."

We sit quietly as we each sip our coffees. Finally, I direct the conversation to the place where I know it's hovering.

"I really appreciate you helping me out by letting me stay here."

"No problem," he says. "You needed a place to stay and we have the room."

"For now. I promise after the holidays, I'll make finding a place my number one priority."

He sighs and sets his empty mug down on the counter behind him. "We're not trying to kick you out, but we're a young married couple. Trying to have a baby. We can't do that with my older brother living down the hall."

"I know. That's why I'll get my own place."

"You have a job now. Even if it's only part-time, you should be able to find an apartment you can afford. There are a couple decent complexes nearby."

"Yeah, I'm picking up extra shifts at the Manor to save until I find something else," I say.

The LeRoy Manor is an upscale entertainment

venue for weddings, parties, and other formal events. I work landscaping, but I'm hoping to get into a more professional position where there's more money. Not exactly my skillset, but apparently what I was doing before wasn't working, so a change was necessary.

"Stay here as long as you need," Michael says. "Don't think we're pushing you out."

"But what happens if Maddie *does* get pregnant?"

"We'll deal with it then. Just keep your eyes out for a place of your own as you go. When the right opportunity comes, you'll know."

My instincts haven't led me anywhere great before. It's one of the reasons why I'm living in a cramped bedroom at my baby brother's house with half of my stuff in storage.

I only hope that when the right opportunity comes, I'll recognize it.

❄ ❄ ❄

EVER SINCE I arrived at work, I've been helping to decorate the whole place for Christmas. Even though there are only twenty days until Christmas, there are six weddings scheduled, three corporate parties, and two charity events. And they all expect this place to look immaculate. Instagram-worthy.

Nearly every pine tree on the property has lights all the way to the top—no matter how tall. Lights have been draped in the branches of the other trees to hide the dead look. And then there's the wreaths hanging on every door, the garland wrapped around step banisters, and the bows under every window.

The decorations have all been planned out: elegant and festive without being over-the-top. Clear lights, not colored lights. Garland and bows, not tinsel and plastic decorations.

By the time the other few guys in the evening crew and I finish, we're tired and cold and trying not to think about the fact that everything will need to come *down* in just four short weeks. Still, even I have to admit that everything looks nice.

I don't even want to think about all the decorating that needs to be done inside.

When I go inside for my break to warm up, I sit down at the plastic table in the small break room. Pulling off my knit hat, I take off my Carhartt jacket and hang it on the hook behind the door.

Just as I'm sucking down half of my water bottle, the door opens and Mr. Woodward, my boss, peeks his head in.

"Hey Jeff, you got a minute?"

I fan out my hands. "I'm on your dime, Mr. Woodward. You have me until second shift is over."

He steps further into the room and takes a seat in the plastic chair across the table from me. It's probably the only time I've seen him in the break room. His gray suit, ironed to perfection, really emphasizes the contrast between the public and private spaces in this building. The break room is painted white, with fluorescent lighting and cheap furniture. A far cry from what would be seen in the main part of the manor.

"On that note," he says. "I wanted to run something by you. A proposition of sorts. Interested?"

I sit up straighter and lean on the table. "Hey, I'm the one who told you I'd love to do some extra work for more cash."

"That's right. And this will help you prove yourself to get you in from out of the cold," he says. "Maybe if I like what I see, you'll be trading those boots of yours for penny loafers."

"Easy now," I say with a laugh. "But seriously, what do you have in mind?"

"Well, one of the upcoming weddings we have scheduled—the Christmas Eve one?" He waits to read my recognition, but scheduling is not something that I'm ever involved with. "Anyway, the bride wants to design her own dessert table. Layout spread, types of desserts, the whole thing."

I reach for another sip of my water. "Isn't that something catering usually takes care of?"

"Well, they're already having the food catered, they'll have an open tab for drinks, and they've already splurged on a number of other upgrades. I think I'll let them slide on the desserts."

"Got it. So what do you want me to do?"

"She needs help."

"Planning the desserts?" I ask with a cocked eyebrow. "You think I can help her with that?"

"Hey, it's a chance," he says. "I'm giving you an opportunity here. Do you want to take it?"

There's that word again.

I sigh. "How long do I have to think about it?"

He checks his watch. "I'll need an answer by…now."

Startled, I say, "But I'm not dressed to meet with a paying customer. Not someone who obviously has money." And someone who is probably very spoiled and judgmental.

"I'll forewarn her about your haggard appearance."

I laugh. "Gee, thanks."

"So it's a deal?"

"How much extra cash are we talking?"

"Double what you're making now, off the books. Just keep track of the hours you spend with her and I'll take your word for it."

"You trust me that much?"

"I'm taking a risk with you, sure, but it's only because I have faith in you." Mr. Woodward holds out his hand. "What do you say?"

Double of minimum wage for a few extra hours? Not beaucoup bucks, but enough to catch my attention.

"How long do I need to work with her?"

"As long as she needs," he says. "Don't leave me hanging here, Jeff."

Finally, I shake his hand. "Deal. When do I start?"

"Excellent!" Mr. Woodward smiles wide. "Her name's Alexis Robbins. She's waiting in the foyer now. Give me a minute and I'll explain your appearance. Next time you meet with her, wear something nice, even if you're not at the Manor."

I nod, suddenly nervous. "Okay."

He leaves and I play on my phone for two minutes, trying to distract myself. After trying to flatten my hair down, I rise to my feet and step into the Manor, nervous that my boots will leave marks all over the pristine carpets.

Opportunity, here I come.

DECEMBER 4TH

***

The Manor is crawling with workers setting up chairs and tables and tablecloths and place settings.

I find a spot in the back hallway and do my best to stay out of everyone's way.

As I wait at the Manor for the guy Mr. Woodward said would be out to help me, I catch up on all the texts I've missed while I was working this morning. Luckily it was only a half day, but still I'm exhausted. And walking out of work to nearly *fifty* text messages between Walt, Prudence, and the wedding planner, Marjorie, all discussing aspects of my own wedding without me hasn't helped.

Isn't the wedding supposed to be all about the bride?

Walt: *Do we really need to invite Aunt Paula? She's been*

having health issues.

Prudence: *Yes, she's been sending you money your whole life. The least you can do is invite her to your wedding.*

Marjorie: *It's getting close! The guest list should be set in stone TODAY!*

Prudence: *Only a few last-minute additions.*

Walt: *Who is Mark Swanson?*

Prudence: *He plays golf with your father at Terry Hills.*

Walt: *I don't think I've ever met him.*

Prudence: *Sure you have. At the charity event for the comfort care home on Liberty Street. Remember, he was the one who brought the wine imported from Tuscany? The kind your father and I had on our honeymoon.*

Walt: *Oh yeah. I remember him. But what about Lillian Grendall?*

Prudence: *I have tea with her every Wednesday.*

Walt: *But I haven't met her.*

Prudence: *I have been talking about you to her since you were a boy. I would like her to be at your wedding.*

Walt: *Okay.*

Prudence: *Alexis, are there any final additions you would like to add?*

Walt: *She's at work right now, Mom.*

Prudence: *Yes, that's right. She mentioned that, didn't she?*

On and on the conversation went in a similar fashion. It would've been the same if I had been keeping up in real time. Clearly, Walt and I didn't get a say in what was going to happen at our wedding, but at least Walt got the courtesy of having things run by him. Me, on the other hand, it's like I'm being punished for having a job.

But hey, at least I get to decide on desserts, one of the most trivial things about planning a wedding. After all, the cake has already been decided on. Who cares what else is offered or how it looks?

Out of all my annoyance with everyone—Prudence for taking over; Walt for giving in—who I'm most annoyed with is myself. Not because I didn't get to sit in on the meetings about guest lists or flowers or even what shops I would look at for my dress. No, what I'm most annoyed with myself over is the fact that for once I'm excited about planning an aspect of this wedding: the desserts.

What does that say about me and my relationship with Walt? I try to tell myself it's just wedding stress and that I really do love Walt and wants to spend the rest of my life with him, but still, the thought that this isn't the best decision I've ever made lingers in my head.

Instead of dwelling on any of it, I channel my anger into my phone. I begin to type out a nasty reply to the group text when I hear footsteps behind me.

"Miss Robbins, this is Jeff Stone," Mr. Woodward says as he approaches with a man wearing khaki overalls and work boots. His hair is matted on the top of his head and sticking up straight in the back. "He will be helping you with your dessert arrangements. If you would, please excuse his appearance. He was just outside working. We need the extra manpower outside to put up all the lights and decorations."

Jeff extends his hand toward me and I hesitate before taking it, looking him up and down as I do.

Mr. Woodward just pulled this guy from his maintenance crew and expected him to know about dessert arrangements? What happened to this place being upscale?

"I'll leave you two to it," Mr. Woodward says. "If you need anything, just give me a call and I'll see what I can do. In the meantime, I have a wedding to get ready for tonight."

When he leaves and it's just me and Jeff, neither of us know what to say.

"So…you're the one who's going to help me?" I ask.

He nods. "Guess so."

I look down at the floor and see that there is dried mud on his boots. It won't stain the rug, but it'll still leave entrails behind. With this kind of disregard for the elegance of this place, my mind races thinking of what kind of nightmare the dessert table will end up being.

Then again, it might be fun to see Walt's mother have a conniption over it…

"Are you a baker?"

"No," he says.

"Oh. So you just do outside work."

He raises his eyebrows and looks me up and down. I'm sure it's only because I did the same to him when he first walked in the room.

"Well, that is why they hired me," he says. "Mostly, that is. Mr. Woodward *is* paying me at least a little something to deal with the headache of helping you."

My mouth goes slack a little as I try to determine if his words were insulting enough to complain about. Instead, I let it slide.

"Anyway," he goes on, "I actually have a bunch of stuff to do today—I'm very busy, you know—so if we could just exchange numbers, I'll give you a call when I have a moment to talk."

I doubt he has a lot of work, but I don't push it. I'm just as glad to get out of here sooner rather than later. Maybe I can convince Walt—to then convince Prudence and Walter the Second—to find someone else to plan the desserts. It shouldn't be the bride's priority anyway.

I read off my number as he adds it to his phone, then pull out mine and wait for his number. Instead, he puts his phone away.

"Aren't you going to give me your number?" I ask.

"I have yours. I'll hit you up when I have a free moment."

"But my wedding is in less than three weeks."

"And we'll get everything done by then," he says. "Trust me."

"How will I get your number?"

"When I reach out to you, you'll have my number. Is a text okay?"

"Uh…yeah, that's fine."

"Cool. Then I'll text you." He turns and walks off, leaving me a little stunned at the exchange.

Who the hell is this guy?

"EVERYTHING OKAY IN here, Isabel?" I ask as I step into the kitchen to refill my glass.

"Dinner will be ready soon, dear."

Isabel is Walt the Second and Prudence's live-in home maker. She cooks, cleans, and runs errands as needed. The worst part is, in an eight bedroom house, they probably hardly even notice she's there.

There are nearly three dozen unfrosted sugar cookies sitting out on a drying rack on the island. Likely the result of Isabel's labors.

"Can I help frost these?" I ask.

"Oh, I can get to those," she says quickly. "Miss Prudence will not like seeing them sitting out."

Through the doorway, we can hear the casual discussions between Walt, his parents, and Marjorie, who they invited for dinner. Cocktails and casual conversation always precede dinner.

It's never not a formal occasion with Walt's parents. Luckily he's not as uptight.

"It's no bother," I tell Isabel. Just as I pull out the frosting and begin applying it to the first cookie on the rack, Walt steps into the room behind me.

"There you are." He comes up behind me and kisses me on the cheek before quickly pulling away. "Does Isabel have you working? She can finish that. That's what my parents pay her for."

My eyes flick up to him and hold his gaze for a minute, daring him to continue talking about Isabel as if she's not in the room. I pick up the next cookie and tell him, "I offered. This is what I enjoy doing."

He sighs. "Okay."

I move on to the third cookie, a tense silence filling the kitchen. I'm determined to let it linger, knowing that the moment I back down, the more I'll be condoning his sometimes rude behavior. Every once in a while I see glimpses of his mother in him and I don't like it.

"So how did today go at LeRoy Manor?" he asks.

Now it's my turn to sigh. "Oh. That. Well, I was thinking, would it be a lot of trouble for someone else to plan the dessert table?"

"I thought you'd like it?"

"I would, it's just…with planning the wedding and getting ready for Christmas and work and—"

"Most of the wedding plans are set," Walt says

over me. "I thought we agreed to have a light Christmas this year in lieu of the wedding? And I already told you, with my job at the law firm and being promoted to partner soon, you could probably quit your job if you wanted to."

He's mentioned that before and I thought it might be the perfect opportunity to open a bakery of my own, but the idea doesn't sit well with me. I'd be using someone else's money to fuel my dream. And it's not like it's a bank loan and it's all business. Walt will be my husband. It'd be personal. Emotions would naturally be involved, especially if the business doesn't do as well as he expects—or worse, it does better than any of us expect. Would he want to turn me into the next Betty Crocker when all I really want to do is spend my days making sweet treats for people in the community?

"Just find someone else to do the desserts, okay?" I move on to the next row of cookies.

"No."

I turn and look at him, a scowl on my face. "No?"

Isabel quietly putters around with the dishes in the sink, probably trying to pretend that she can't hear our conversation.

"Lexi, you love to bake." He indicates the half-frosted cookie in my hand. "Obviously. You can't help yourself."

"So you're going to put me to work?"

"No, I'm trying to make sure you have something

that you can take ownership of with this wedding." He takes the cookie from me and sets it back on the tray, turning me to face him. He sets his hands on my shoulders, then rubs my arms awkwardly. "I know my parents—my mother—has been making a lot of decisions for this wedding. And I know it's hard with your mom not being here, so I want to make sure you have something that's yours. I just want to see you happy."

I stare into his eyes, trying to determine if he's being genuine. There's nothing but sincerity looking back at me. If one thing's for certain, Walt loves me. And it's true, he is probably just trying to do what will make me happy.

Too bad he wasn't there to witness my encounter with Jeff. And complaining about it now would seem petty and childish. I can suck it up and work with Jeff for a little while to plan one small aspect of the wedding. After all, twenty days from now the only guy I'll be concerned about will be Walt.

"Okay," I relent. "I'll take care of the desserts. But if your mother complains…"

He laughs and raises his hands in surrender. "She won't! I'll make sure of it."

Isabel chuckles under her breath. Walt and I both look over at her and grin. We all know Prudence always has something to say.

DECEMBER 5TH

Jeff

❄ ❄ ❄

Before I even step foot into the kitchen, I can smell the bacon and eggs frying in the pan and the coffee percolating in the pot. It's Michael's weekly tradition: have a home-cooked breakfast with the family, which includes anyone living in the house.

Back when he was in college his fraternity brothers picked on him for insisting they all eat together every Sunday morning. It was an uphill battle to convince them to get up in time after an evening of partying or some other "extra-curricular" activity. However, the food soon changed their minds. By his senior year, there were people requesting to be in the same housing as him just so they could have their Sunday breakfasts.

Just another way my brother and I are different. I

wouldn't have even thought of sharing that tradition with friends. It was something I had considered starting before—

"Morning!" Maddie says brightly from the top of a chair in the kitchen doorway. She has a small strip of tape stuck to her index finger and a Christmas card in her free hand. The doorway is already adorned with several of them, from the top right down to the floor.

"Morning." I step through the doorway and into the kitchen. Right away, I go straight to the coffee pot.

As expected, Michael is at the stove, shaking the skillet with pizzazz. He's in sweatpants and a hoodie—no formal Sundays here. The added flair today is the Santa hat on the top of his head.

"There you are!" he says with a smile when he sees me. "I was beginning to think you weren't getting up."

"And miss the free food? No chance." I fill my cup of coffee and carry it to the table.

"Isn't every meal here free food? It's not like you're paying rent." He flashes me a smile, then changes the subject because he knows I feel guilty about not being able to give them something for letting me stay here. "Are you feeling better today?"

I stir in the sugar and creamer. "When wasn't I feeling good?"

"Last night," he says. "You came home kind of grumpy."

I can see Maddie nodding from the doorway.

"Well." I take a careful sip of my doctored coffee to determine whether I'm going to have a burnt tongue all day or not. And to buy time. Mostly to buy time. "It was just something that happened at work, that's all."

"Did they cut your hours?" Michael turns off the stove and grabs a plate from the cupboard. "These are ready, hon."

Maddie tapes up the card in her hand and then moves the chair back to the table. She comes over to help her husband. He passes her two plates loaded with food and she carries them over to the table, setting one in front of me. Michael soon joins with the third plate and several forks for everyone.

"No, Mr. Woodward actually gave me more hours…sort of."

"Sort of?" Maddie asks. "What does that mean?"

"It means…" I sigh and take a bite of the bacon. Nice and crunchy. "So there's this wedding there Christmas Eve —"

"He wants you to work Christmas Eve?" Michael asks. "I thought we were having our own little party here before we go to Mom and Dad's on Christmas Day?"

"We are," I say. "I'm not working the wedding, just preparing for it. He knows how I'm kind of desperate to save money and all, so he said he'd pay me extra to help this lady plan the desserts for her wedding."

Michael snickers. "What do you know about desserts?"

"Nothing," I admit. "But I think Mr. Woodward's thinking I can help with the arrangement because of my background."

Maddie nods as she stabs the next bite on her plate. "I think you'd be good at that. You have an eye for what looks good."

"Thanks."

"Not seeing a reason you should be grumpy here," Michael says.

I scoop up the last of my eggs and chew. Again, buying time. The more I think about my altercation with Lexi—and my sour attitude the rest of the night—the more I feel like I'm being childish. But I wasn't the one who set the tone for our meeting, so at least I have some ground to stand on when it comes to justifying my response.

"I met the girl yesterday—Lexi—and she was just the LeRoy Manor type," I start. "You know, fancy outfit, heels, attention buried in her phone, the whole nine yards."

"You should be used to it by now," Michael says.

"He's never had to work directly with them before," Maddie tells him in my defense.

"Right. So anyway, Mr. Woodward kind of told

me at the last minute when I was on my break—literally five minutes before I met her. I spent the first half of my shift setting up decorations outside, so I wasn't really dressed to be mingling with everyone inside. I realized when I followed him to the public area that I had left a trail of dirt, so I had to clean that up before anyone stepped in it."

"The glamorous life of a maintenance worker," Michael says with a grin. He sets his fork down on his empty plate and leans back in his chair with his coffee—likely not his first of the morning.

"Was this Lexi girl stuck-up?" Maddie asks.

"Uh, that would be putting it nicely," I say. "She looked me up and down, judging me in an instant, shocked that I was the one they had sent to help her. She probably thought that I was that thing that lives under the porch that someone keeps feeding. That's the way she looked at me. Probably wondering what she and her rich fiancé are paying for. Probably thinks—"

Michael holds up his hand to stop me. "We get it. It was embarrassing. So?"

I look at him with wide eyes. "So I wasn't going to let her treat me like that."

"Jeff, she's the customer," he says.

"As rude as she is, sometimes you have to suck it up," Maddie admits.

I sigh. "She wasn't *rude*, necessarily. I mean, kind of, but not blatantly. Anyway, I'm going to talk to Mr.

Woodward tomorrow to see if I can get out of it. I have a feeling the interaction I had yesterday with Lexi is going to be the same every time we see each other."

"You don't know that," Michael says.

"Yeah, she could've just been having a bad day," Maddie offers.

"Besides, Mr. Woodward is just trying to give you a chance," he adds. "Don't turn it down because then there might not be other opportunities like this."

"That's true."

Great, I think. *They're tag-teaming me.*

"Besides," Maddie says. "How long is it *really* going to take to plan out the desserts? Like one, maybe two meetings tops? The sooner you get it over with, the sooner you'll be done working with her."

I sigh again. "I guess that's true."

"Just don't rule it out," Michael says. "You never know how it'll play out. First impressions aren't everything."

That may be the case, but I have a bad feeling about this one. No matter what I tell Michael and Maddie to get the conversation to end, I'm still going to talk to Mr. Woodward tomorrow. I don't know if I'll be able to stand even one or two meetings with Little Miss Lexi.

❄ ❄ ❄

❄ RIGHT WHEN I get to work the next day, I go straight to Mr. Woodward's office. I'm working the day shift, so he's just arrived as well. It's the perfect opportunity to talk to him before he gets started with his day.

"Jeffrey!" he exclaims with a smile when he sees me step into the doorway of the small office. His mood is always better before the stress of the day gets to him — another reason to talk to him early. "How are you this morning?"

"Not bad. You got a minute?"

He pulls the empty office chair next to him out and motions for me to take a seat. "You got any decorations up at your house?"

I nod. "Yeah, I helped my brother put up lights outside his and his wife's house. They went and got a tree the day after Thanksgiving and yesterday we put up more lights."

Mr. Woodward laughs. "It never ends, does it? My wife is obsessed with elves. Stuffed ones, porcelain ones, creepy ones, you name it. We've got it. Makes Christmas shopping for her easy, but man what I wouldn't give to toss out half of them."

"Yeah, I bet. Look, I wanted to talk to you about something."

"What's on your mind?"

"I met with Lexi on Saturday — the Christmas Eve bride."

Mr. Woodward's face lightened with recognition. "Ah, the one with the dessert thingy. How'd it go?"

"Well…" I pause, again trying to figure out how best to work it so I don't come off like a whiny brat.

Am I being a whiny brat?

"I don't feel like we really…connected, I guess," I finally say. "Like there was this awkward tension between us."

Mr. Woodward waves it off. "I've dealt with all kinds of people in this business. You don't always *click* with all of them. All that matters is if they're satisfied."

"Right, but I'm not sure she'll be satisfied after working with me."

"So what are you saying?"

"I was just wondering if there was anyone else you had in mind to work with her."

Mr. Woodward studies me, then crosses his arms and leans back in his chair. "You know, I know your situation. I know you've fallen on some hard times—and I feel for you. I also know you're trying to better yourself. I'm just trying to help you with that."

"I know, and I appreciate that, but I just feel like—"

"Like you want to quit? Because that's what it sounds like to me. That you're quitting at this opportunity I'm giving you before it gets too hard. Before you even get started. Before you've even given it a chance."

My blood starts to boil. I am *not* a quitter. This is just a different situation. Lexi isn't someone I can see myself working with—not someone I think I'll be able to *stand* working with. But that's not going to convince Mr. Woodward. He has a business to run and I'm making things more complicated for him during a very busy month.

"I'm just saying, I'd like to see you give this an honest effort," he continues. "Don't forfeit the game before you've even had a chance to play." He grins. "Heard that in a movie once and thought it was very poignant."

Slowly, I nod, conceding to the fact that Lexi is someone I'm going to have to see at least one more time before I can be done with her. And luckily, I know Mr. Woodward will be gracious enough not to remind me of this moment of weakness.

When I leave the office, I step into the break room and pull out my phone. Bringing up Lexi's number, I type out a quick text: *Hey Lexi, it's Jeff from LeRoy Manor. Let me know what day works best to meet up. Thanks.*

Short, sweet, and to the point. And, as an added cherry on top, very polite.

Hopefully I get the same tone in return. Otherwise, it's going to be a long time to Christmas.

DECEMBER 9TH
Lexi

❄ ❄ ❄

"Here you go," Jeff tells me as he sets a glass of water in front of me on the large conference table. A second later, he passes me a cocktail napkin to serve as a coaster.

"Thanks." I pull out some papers from the folder I brought with me. Print outs from different dessert table displays I found on Pinterest. I figured I should come to this meeting with *something*.

"Are these your ideas?" He slides one of the papers closer to himself to look.

"Yeah, I guess. Just some things I found online that I like. I'm not partial to anyone in particular, really."

He reaches for another one. "No, this is a good start."

I sit quietly as he looks at each of the papers I

brought. It was strange to walk into the Manor and have it be nearly empty. I figured there would be a company party or a wedding or something going on here, but Jeff said it's still early in the month for a lot of holiday parties—never mind the fact that my future in-laws are hosting one tomorrow night at their house. And, Jeff pointed out, Thursdays are kind of a slow day for event venues anyway.

"All right, this is good," Jeff says suddenly. He opens his own folder and pulls out three different sheets of paper—all seem to be hand-drawn sketches. "This first one is a much more practical approach. Kind of a buffet-style, but still quite appealing to the eye. This second one really puts the cake at the centerpiece, however, this would eliminate any other kinds of desserts to make the cake the focus. And it would require an additional staff member to cut pieces for everyone, so that's something to think about. This third option is a bit off-the-wall. I thought it'd be cool to feature non-traditional desserts like donuts or scones."

"So breakfast foods?" I ask with a scoff. "Have you met Walt's mother? She wouldn't ever go for that. And the buffet style would work at some weddings, but again, I don't think Prudence would like it."

"What do *you* like? Have you guys finalized what types of desserts you'll have available yet?"

"That's what this meeting is about, isn't it?"

Jeff pulls out another sheet of paper, this one listing prices. "Let's see here...um, you guys are getting the pink champagne wedding cake, right?"

I shrug. "I guess so." That was one of those decisions that was made with me present, but not an active part of the decision.

"So we should look for desserts that complement that. Um..." He looks in his folder for any additional paperwork that can help him sound like he knows what he's talking about.

Based on this meeting, my first guess is right: they pulled this guy from outside and stuck him with me. Neither Walt's parents nor the workers at the Manor want to deal with me. And here I was foolishly believing that the bride got her way at the wedding.

"So pink champagne has a, uh, champagne taste, but it's also usually paired with strawberry or...something..." He murmurs while looking over his list of prices. "Would chocolate work?"

I sigh. "Yes, I think that could work. Typically, if you have a specific taste like pink champagne, it's probably a better option to have an alternative for the people who don't like that unique option. So chocolate would work, but it depends on what kind. We're not going to have a whole other cake there, and cupcakes are out of the question. We could do truffles, but those would be more expensive." Not that a cost was ever an issue with this wedding, but perhaps it would be if I was the one suggesting the price increases.

"Well, it's up to you. We can do an ice cream bar or cake pops or—"

My head began shaking before he even finished the first suggestion. "Ice cream is too messy. Cake pops aren't elegant enough. I'm thinking like macarons or simple little cookies—nothing too large."

"Are you, like, a baker or something?" Jeff asks suddenly.

Now it's my turn to stammer. "Um…not technically, although I do love to bake."

"Are you any good?"

Another very direct, abrupt question. I scan his face to try to determine his intent, but I don't see any malice behind it. Maybe Jeff is just one of those people who isn't aware of how abrasive he can be.

"I think so," I mutter, then quickly add, "Anyway, I'm surprised you don't know some of these things yourself. Doesn't your wife or girlfriend bake?"

Jeff sits up straighter, as if recoiling back into his turtle shell. "I'm not married and I'm not seeing anyone," he says briskly, all the lightness from his voice gone.

Apparently, somewhere along the way I touched a nerve. "It's really the display that I'm struggling with," I finally say in an effort to get the conversation back on track. "I can choose the desserts myself. I'm just not sure how I want them arranged." I reach for one of the sketches that he pulled out of his folder earlier. "These all look nice, but I'm thinking of something more like—" Reaching for a sheet I brought, I set it beside Jeff's. "—this. Maybe these two combined. Something like that. Does that make sense?"

He reaches for a blank sheet of paper and a pencil. "Okay, so something like—" Bringing pencil to paper, he quickly sketches out a table with a dessert display that matches what we'd both been discussing. In a matter of a minute, he took an empty page and created something that looked perfect. "—this. Maybe we could come up with some fancy tablecloth or something too to match the colors of the rest of the wedding—white and green, right?"

My eyes are wide and I stare at the sketch a little dumbfounded. "You just *drew* that?"

He can't keep back his smile and he uses the pencil to adjust some details that are invisible to me. "Yeah, so does this look good?"

"Are you an artist or something? Just working here to make money on the side?"

"Something like that," he says.

I stare at the image, pulling it closer for a better look.

"I like to draw," he tells me. "I first got into it as a kid when I was obsessed with comic books—as geeky as that makes me sound. I loved the illustrations and tried to do it myself. It just kind of grew from there and I developed my own style, I guess."

"This is amazing."

"Thanks," he says. "So my childhood obsession resulted in *something* good. Drawing. And reading, too."

Another surprise. I didn't peg him for a reader. I look up at him and stare in his brown eyes, wondering what other secrets he's holding in there. "I like to read too."

He smiles. "What are you reading now?"

"*A Christmas Carol* by Charles Dickens. I read it every year. I try to find different adaptations to keep it fresh, but reading the story itself is a holiday tradition of mine. What are you reading?"

"Um, a biography on Bill Gates. I like to read stories on people who have been very successful in life. See if there's anything they're doing that I can emulate."

"Very cool," I say, still in shock that he had these talents and interests that I never would've thought he'd have. My smile dampens a bit as I realize how judgmental that makes me. "The one good thing about Walt's parents is that they have this library in their house. It's not a big room, but the whole thing is lined with bookshelves filled with books they've honestly probably never read. There are comfortable seats in there, blankets, plenty of natural light. It's the perfect reading den—something I'd love to have in my own house someday."

"That's cool."

I nod and look down at the sketches Jeff drew. "Yeah."

That aspiration for the future is definitely within my grasp by marrying Walt and his money, but the bigger part of that picture of a home library is sharing it with someone who likes to read as much as me. Someone who is okay with comfortable silence every now and then. Someone who isn't so caught up with appearances, who is willing to indulge in baked goods because it's made by someone who loves them. Someone who is a complement to my own life and interests.

"I'm going to be honest here," Jeff says. "You are completely surprising me."

"How's that?"

"Well, I see the people who get married here. The types of brides who show up. I've seen the full gambit, from bridezilla to go-with-the-flow types. None of them are like you."

I recoil a little with a smile. "Is that a good thing?"

"Oh yeah. Definitely. But it's still surprising. You have the opportunity to have this huge wedding and you just seem to not care about having an extravagant day."

I chip off the nail polish on my fingernails. I'll have to repaint them anyway before the party tomorrow. "To be honest, Walt's wealth is kind of foreign to me. It kind of makes me uncomfortable. Sometimes with his family I feel like an outsider."

"All the time?"

"Usually." I sigh. "I thought it'd be different once I started to become more of a permanent fixture in Walt's life, but so far that hasn't been the case."

"Have you brought this up to Walt?"

"Yeah, and things with him have been better since then. But we've been spending more time with his family lately because of the wedding planning and I just feel more and more…pushed aside."

"So are you sure you should even be getting married?"

Our eyes meet, both of us unsure of how to proceed. How we got on this topic to begin with. Jeff's question hangs in the air. Although it's been floating on the outskirts of my conscious thoughts for a while, I've never heard it said out loud before. Now that I have, I'm not sure how to react.

My phone rings and I jump to my feet. Walt's smiling face appears on the screen of my phone.

"This is Walt," I say quickly. My shaky hands wave in the air, over-gesturing due to my discomfort. "It's getting late. I have to go."

"Oh. Okay." Jeff begins to collect my papers for me.

"Keep those. I'm just—I have to leave now." I grab my coat and hook one arm through, my other arm holding the phone to my ear to answer.

I'm not sure what just happened in that conference room, but it's a good thing it's over.

Friday, December 10th

THE PIANIST PLAYS a mellow version of "Winter Wonderland" in the formal living room, which mixes with the sound of discussions and clinking glasses throughout the house. Each doorway is lined with garland and red bows. The garland running down the staircase banister is lit up with white lights. The formal living room and dining room—both of which are situated at the front of the house with large Palladian windows—are adorned with Christmas trees that were decorated and staged by someone from Buffalo that Prudence and Walter the Second had hired. No string of popcorn or homemade ornaments here.

Meanwhile, I'm standing in a green cocktail dress beside Walt, nursing a glass of champagne, which doesn't even taste that good. Walt is currently in discussion with someone he does business with. Mr. Dorschel or something. His wife looks equally as bored as I am.

"Yeah, we try to go up to the lake at least once a month when it's warm," Dorschel was saying. "We have a time share over on Seneca Lake. It's nice to get away, spend time on the boat, stop at the wineries—just relax, you know?"

Walt nods. "That sounds great. I would love to get something like that for me and Lexi, but between buying a house, remodeling, and the wedding, a vacation house is going to have to be put on the back burner for now. Maybe next year." He hooks his arm around me. "What do you think? First anniversary present to ourselves?"

Isn't the first anniversary gift supposed to be related to paper? A second home seems like a big jump. Still, I raise my eyebrows and smile politely.

Truth be told, I'm only partially listening. Part of me is taking in the crowd, sizing up the other guests—lawyers, doctors, city councilmen, and Tracy Slater and her husband. Can't leave out Batavia's biggest success, not if everyone will be talking about how *wonderful* this Christmas party was.

Inside, I roll my eyes at the lengths my future in-laws would go for the sake of appearance.

Another part of me is still thinking about Jeff. Or rather, the question I left unanswered last night. All day long I've been kicking myself for leaving him with the assumption that I'm having doubts about my upcoming marriage.

Of course I'm positive that I want to marry Walt. He is everything that I need in life: someone who treats me well, who can take care of me, and who's easy on the eyes. All that other stuff about the money and feeling left out is just pre-wedding jitters. The nerves anyone feels about fitting in with someone else's family before they begin to feel like your own.

Marrying Walt is the right choice.

Speaking of him, I'm pulled out of my thoughts as he tugs on my arm.

"Come on, Lex. My mother's calling for us."

I look across the room and see Prudence waving daintily our way. She turns back to a portly man in a suit coat whose seams are working overtime to stay together.

"Walter!" he cheers as he grabs Walt's hand and draws him in for a quick hug. "It's so nice to see you! Merry Christmas!"

"Merry Christmas, Pastor Sampson." Walt turns to me and motions to Sampson. "He's going to be officiating the wedding."

"Oh!" I reach for his hand and display another polite smile. At least meeting the man who will help make me a wife two weeks before the wedding is better than meeting him the day of. Yet another decision made without me, but it's only an officiant, right?

"The big day's coming up," Sampson says. "Are you all prepared?"

"I believe so," Prudence answers, as if she's the one about to walk down the aisle. "Some details are still being finalized." She turns to me. "Which reminds me, how are you doing planning the dessert table?"

Her eyes seem to bore into me, as if suggesting why I haven't moved quicker on an assignment I've only had about a week to do. Luckily, I have a ready response for her out of sheer luck.

"Actually, I met with someone at the Manor last night about it. We went over some options, talked about the display. It's going to look really nice."

"Just remember that the wedding is only two weeks away."

I force a smile. "Oh, I'm very aware of when my wedding is. Rest assured, it will be done on time."

"Well, I think this is a great party!" Sampson says suddenly, cutting into the growing tension. "The place looks beautiful, Prudence. You've really outdone yourself."

She hasn't done a thing, other than swipe that credit card.

"I'm running to the bathroom," I murmur to Walt.

He takes my glass of champagne and watches me leave.

Down the hall, away from the noise—and stress—of the party, I immediately feel myself begin to relax. Thanks to Jeff, I can't help but wonder if this is the type of escape I'm going to need during every holiday for the rest of my life. On the bright side, Walt is ten years older than me, which means his parents are older, so they probably only have a few —

No, I'm not going to wish Walt's parents dead. I need to find a way to deal with them without losing my mind. Who knew that the hardest part of marrying someone was their parents?

As I reach for the door to the bathroom, it suddenly swings inward and I jump back in surprise as someone exits.

"Oh! I'm sorry!" Tracy Slater says with a genuine smile.

Now here's a woman who can sympathize with what Walt's probably going through: finding someone who cares about you and not about your wealth. Word around town is that Tracy's first husband was more interested in her money than her.

"No, it's my fault," I stammer. "I didn't realize anyone was in there."

"No problem," she says, then turns to make her way down the hall.

On a whim, I call out her name. "Tracy?"

She turns. "Yes?"

"Um…" I hesitate, but decide I'm too far in now to take it back. "Pardon my asking, but are you…happy with Steven?" She and her current husband married very quickly after her divorce. And they even started a family. Her music career has slowed down a bit, but she's stated in interviews that she's happier now. Hopefully that's not just some PR baloney. And if she's being honest, maybe she can help me figure out how to tell if you're marrying someone for the right reasons.

Damn you, Jeff, for making me doubt myself like this.

"Of course, very much so," Tracy says easily. "Why do you ask?"

Suddenly, I feel dumb. Why can't I figure out my feelings on my own? At the very least, I shouldn't have to bring a stranger into my world of self-doubt. The problem is, most people are strangers to me.

"It's nothing," I say with a disarming grin. "Forget I asked."

Tracy doesn't leave. Instead, she takes a step forward and reaches for my hand. "Speaking as a woman who once married the wrong man, if you're having *any* doubts about walking down the aisle, you shouldn't do it. Deep down, you know the right path forward. Only you can make that call."

My mouth has suddenly gone dry and I stare blankly at her. Does she know Jeff? Have they been talking about me behind my back? Trying to get me to leave Walt for some reason?

The absurdity of that idea immediately dismisses the thought from my mind, but still, it's eerie that within the span of twenty-four hours, I've had two people allude to the fact that I'm about to make a mistake. *Two weeks* before my wedding.

"Hey, Lex," Walt says from the end of the hall. "The Johansons are leaving and want to say goodbye."

I clear my throat, forcing myself to break out of my train of thought. "Okay."

Pulling my hand away from Tracy's, I step around her and back into the party. Once again, I leave the warning unanswered.

DECEMBER 11TH
Jeff

✳ ✳ ✳

Just after I turn off the water in the shower, my phone starts ringing from where it sits on the bathroom vanity. Grabbing the towel from the hook, I quickly dry off and wrap it around myself, answering the phone at the last ring.

"Hello?"

"Hey, are you busy?" It's Lexi.

"Uh, not really. What's up?" Hopefully she doesn't ask me to meet with her again. I got most of what I needed the other day. As much as I wouldn't mind seeing more of Lexi—she turned out to be different than I had originally thought—I was hoping to spend my day off Christmas shopping, which I haven't even started yet.

"You sound out of breath," she says.

"Just caught off guard, I guess."

"Oh. Well, listen, is there any way we could speed along the plans we discussed on Thursday? Yesterday, Walt's family had this Christmas party and they were bugging me about getting everything finalized because the wedding is in less than two weeks and I don't know how much longer I can hold them off." She laughs, but I can tell her question is genuine.

"Um…I think I have a lot of what I need already," I tell her. "I can put it all together and go over it with you. Maybe give you some sketches for you to give Walt's family to convince them we're on the right track."

"Thanks! When can we go over that? I actually have the morning off for once, so I'm free all day. Except, I would prefer to stay in Batavia. Someplace I can walk to. Not that LeRoy's far, but it's just the matter of getting in the car and going." Another nervous laugh. "Unless, of course, you don't live in town. Then I can meet you somewhere."

"No, I'm here in town too," I tell her. I lean against the vanity and stare down at the tiled floor, debating my options. I suppose I could go Christmas shopping tomorrow. I was planning on laying on the couch and watching the football game, but if I go in the morning, I should be back by the afternoon. "You want to meet at a restaurant downtown? Maybe over lunch?"

Did I just ask a soon-to-be-married woman on a date? A *lunch* date at that.

She groans on the other end. "Erm…"

"Unless you had another idea in mind," I add quickly.

"Well, it's just that I've been trying to cut back on my extra expenses with the wedding coming up and all," Lexi says. "I know, it's kind of stupid with all the money Walt's family has, but I want to be able to pay my own way, to a certain degree, and all of these costs are really adding up."

"No, that makes sense. So if you don't want to go out somewhere and you don't want to go to the Manor, where else is there?" The library comes to my mind, but I don't offer it since it's not exactly downtown. Still within walking distance to downtown, but off the beaten path a bit.

"You could come to my apartment," she offers. "I'll bake."

"Are you sure?" How did we jump from a lunch date to going straight to her house?

"Yeah, it'll be fine. I live right downtown on Jackson. Above the old *Daily News* building. I'll make some of my Christmas cookies and you can decide for yourself if I'm a good baker."

I laugh nervously. "Okay, sure. Twelve o'clock?"

"I'll be here."

❄ ❄ ❄

AS I CLIMB the steps to the official front door of Lexi's apartment, my mind swirls with fears that I'm crossing a major line here. I'm only supposed to be helping her with one small part of her wedding, not making house calls. Would Mr. Woodward fire me for this? Or worse, will Walt not like this?

But then, Lexi invited me herself. And for all I know, Walt is here too and I can go over the plans with both of them and then be on my way.

That thought doesn't seem to do anything to keep my heart from racing.

Lexi opens the door with a smile, wrapped in a red and white apron smeared with flour. I'm immediately hit with the delicious smell of baking. More notably, it's warm inside, but not stifling. Cozy and very homely.

"You made it!" she says. "Can I take your coat?"

"Sure." I set the folder I brought with me down and shrug out of my coat. "Honestly, I probably didn't even need it. It's been so warm out lately."

"I know," she says with a groan. "I heard it's supposed to be fifty degrees today and rainy. Walt and I were hoping for a white Christmas wedding."

"There's still two more weeks, so you never know."

She hangs my coat on the rack behind the door. "I know."

Her apartment is bigger than I thought it'd be. To the right is the living room with two large windows overlooking Jackson Street. To the left is the kitchen, with a small center island and stainless steel appliances. Lexi moves behind it and continues cleaning up the mess from the baking. With the high ceilings, she looks so small in the space, which isn't that big in reality. Across the room there's a doorway that opens to a small hallway leading to what I presume is the bedroom and bathroom.

"Take a seat." She indicates the barstools by the island. When I sit, she hands me a cookie still hot from the oven. "Try it. Tell me what you think and be brutally honest."

I take a bite and the gingerbread immediately brings a wave of nostalgia. My mother used to make these all the time when Michael and I were growing up. Just one bite brings back memories of playing in the snow with the Christmas lights glowing or the smell of the wood-burning stove my dad always stoked up or the excitement that built as the anticipation ate away at me waiting for Christmas to arrive.

"This is fantastic."

"Really?" She flashes a bright smile.

"Add some cream cheese frosting and this is perfection."

"Funny you should mention that." She turns and sets a carton of Pillsbury frosting in front of me. "I usually make my own frosting, but this year I cheated with everything I've got going on."

I open the carton and dip a piece of the gingerbread in before taking another bite. "Lex, this is so good. Seriously, you should be running a bakery."

Instantly, her smile fades and she busies herself with tidying again. "I'd love that, but to be honest, I'm kind of afraid to."

"Afraid? Of what? You'll have people lining out the door for these!"

"Maybe, but what if they don't? I mean, I work at a bank and I see people every day come in for business loans only to see them turned away or watch as their business closes down after a couple years. I just don't want to fail at something I'm so passionate about. I'd rather daydream about the possibility."

I sigh. "You know, I was one of those business owners who failed."

Her head snaps up to me. "You were?"

"I don't talk about it much, but yeah. That's why I'm working at the Manor. To help rebuild what I lost when my business went under."

"I'm so sorry."

"It's okay. I had a comic shop in Rochester, which was supposed to be my savior, but it was in a bad location—the best I could get for the rent I could afford—and it kept getting vandalized. Finally, I had to concede to the fact that I wasn't making any money off of it. I closed it and moved in with my brother and his wife. That was just over the summer.

So you're not really catching me at my best, actually."

"Oh, Jeff, that stinks," she says. "But…what did you mean when you said the shop was supposed to be your savior? What were you doing before that?"

"I was working maintenance at O-AT-KA, which was okay, but not my dream job."

"So what made you decide to take the leap?"

I let out a deep breath, debating whether I should reveal yet another part of my life that I've been keeping quiet for several years now. But Lexi isn't asking to pry. She's asking because she cares, even if we've only known each other for a week.

"About five years ago, my wife passed away."

"Oh."

"She had cancer and was sick for a while," I went on. "We were always talking about *someday*. Someday we'll go to Europe. Someday we'll have a family. Someday I'll learn to enjoy life. When she died, I took that as a sign that I needed to make someday happen sooner than later. I'd been dreaming about opening a bookstore of some kind for a while and I got to know the owner of the shop in Rochester, just by being a patron. He was looking to retire and offered to sell me the business for a good price. So I took it."

"Jeff, I'm so sorry about your wife."

"It's okay. Alice is still with me." Digging into my shirt, I pull at the chain necklace and reveal the wedding band at the end. "Seemed silly to wear it with her gone, but I still couldn't bring myself to lock it in a box somewhere. Anyway, the neighborhood the comic shop was in used to be a nice family-friendly area when he first opened it, but over the years the neighborhood turned and it only got worse the longer I was there."

"So you had the business for a couple years then?"

I nod. "Almost five years."

"Then that's not a failure in my book! You were following your dream for five years! Now you just need to figure out the next dream. Maybe another comic shop or bookstore or something."

I look up at her with a grin. "Coming from the woman who is afraid to open a bakery."

"Touché." She smiles at me, then says, "You know what we need?"

"What's that?"

"To get out of our heads for a while. What were you planning on doing today?"

"Christmas shopping," I tell her. "Haven't started yet."

"Me neither! Granted, I don't really have anyone to buy for, but still. We should go do that!"

"Together?"

"Why not? It's better than sitting here and eating our weight in cookies and wallowing about missed — and ignored — opportunities."

I laugh. "Okay then, sure."

She pulls off her apron, pulls the hair tie out of her hair, and steps toward the front door. "Hope you brought your list with you."

"It's all up here." I point to my head.

We put on our jackets and head out onto the sidewalk. It's warm and the gloom of the day has finally relented to rain. We each pull up our hoods to protect us from the inevitable.

"Come on, let's cut through Jackson Square," she says, leading me into the alley beside her building.

The alley opens up to the back end of several buildings lining nearby streets. There's another building here that used to be a warehouse and is now apartments. Beside it is a stage where they do concerts in the summer. Between the vines clinging to the historic brick walls are murals painted by the city's artists over the years. Portrayals of businesses that once lined Main Street, painted windows with flower boxes, advertisements for current businesses on Center Street. It's a representation of a community from years ago until now.

"This is my favorite place in town," she tells me. "I love that it's old, I love that it's still used, and I love that people have been slowly adding their artwork here."

"It's definitely an under-appreciated part of the city."

Lexi slowly moves through the square, looking at the murals with a close eye, ignoring the raindrops falling down around us giving the air a damp chill.

I'm also taken by the murals, staring at the details of a painted storefront with the words "Library and Reading Rooms" painted on the second floor.

"Are you coming?"

I turn and notice Lexi is walking down the alley toward Center Street. Running to catch up, I stop hard beside her, accidentally splashing water from a puddle on her.

My eyes grow wide with worry that I just ruined her day, but instead her mouth turns up into a laugh.

"You did that on purpose!" She stomps her own foot down in the puddle in an attempt to splash me, but I jump back in time. "Don't run away from me!"

I backpedal back into Jackson Square and stop beside a rather large puddle. Lexi stands on the other side, both of us sizing the other up.

She fakes left, then goes right. I start to run toward her, only to jump into the middle of the puddle, sending water up at my legs, but also toward Lexi. She yelps with a giggle and jumps back. When she looks at me, she bursts out laughing.

The puddle was deeper than I thought. Both my feet are completely submerged in the water.

"Didn't think that one out very well, did you?"

I laugh and slowly step out of the water, shaking as much as I can out of my shoes. It's useless.

"Do you want to go home to dry off?" she suggests.

I shrug, not wanting to put an end to this outing with her. "I'll manage, even if I'm a little squishy."

"It's Christmas, who isn't?"

I decide to let the comment slide and lead her back toward Center Street. She leads me into the toy store, which is likely one of the oldest businesses in the area.

"Hi Adam," Lexi says to the owner with a smile.

"Merry Christmas! Is there something I can help you guys find?"

"No, I think I'll be okay," she says. "I'll let you know if I need anything, though."

We move to the back room where there are bicycles lined up along the back wall.

"I thought you said you didn't have very many people to shop for?" I ask. "Or are you shopping for yourself?"

She smirks. "Actually, I've been known to come in here to get some puzzles from time to time."

"You like to do puzzles?"

"Is there something wrong with that?"

I put up my hands in surrender. "Not at all. Just surprised."

"They help me relax. Between that and reading, it's how I unwind from the day. I don't really watch TV." She stops in front of a cookware set with a small stove and oven. "I like to buy a gift or two each year and donate it to a local church or something that's doing a toy drive for kids who wouldn't get a

Christmas otherwise. I'd love to buy something big like this but it's out of my price range." She looks at it longingly before moving on.

"Next year you'll be able to."

She looks up at me, confused. "What'll be different about next year?"

"Doesn't your future husband have money? You guys could sponsor a whole family or something. Not to sound immature, but you're about to be rich."

She shrugs and moves on to inspect a mystery date game. "It'll be my husband's money, not mine. And besides, that's something I still haven't wrapped my head around yet. I'm always going to have buyer's remorse, for everything I buy. No matter how much money I have."

"But your circumstances are changing, so maybe your way of thinking will too."

"It just feels off because I've never had money." She sets the box back on the shelf and moves over to an area full of stuffed animals.

"Oh, come on, we all feel like we're broke, but we're doing better than we think," I say. "And this is coming from a guy who is currently living with his little brother."

"At least you have a place to go."

"What does that mean?"

"It means...not all of us are like that. Some people *don't* have a roof over their heads."

I stop and look at her. Her words seem to be

coming from personal experience.

My silence makes her take notice. She looks back at me and sighs. "Look, I'm only going to tell you this because you told me something incredibly personal about your life and I trust that you're going to keep this to yourself."

All I can do is nod, feeling like the biggest jerk for having put my foot in my mouth. It's like I twisted her arm to tell me something she wanted to keep to herself. I, of all people, should know what that's like.

"Lexi, you don't have to—"

"My mom and I didn't have a lot of money when I was younger," she says over me. "Honestly, looking back, it's probably a good possibility that she was doing drugs. Not a lot, she still kept a part-time job, but there are signs that I now recognize as patterns of substance abuse."

"That must've been hard." I try to create an image in my mind of the things she must've experienced. Being left home alone, not having very much food, not having a Christmas. I realize that all of these images are things I've only pulled from books or movies. I've never actually been in that situation so I have no idea what she's experienced. Besides, she's already sharing enough about her life. I don't want to pry.

"Anyway," she goes on, "when I was about thirteen, we were evicted from our apartment around Halloween. My mother promised we'd be back in a home of our own by Christmas—and she really worked hard to get there—but it just didn't work out in time."

"Where did you go?"

"We were staying at a hotel out by the thruway," she says. "It was only until maybe February, but that meant that I didn't really get a Christmas that year. One of the teachers at school found out about our situation and made arrangements to have gifts delivered, which was generous and humiliating at the same time. Either way, if it wasn't for someone caring about me and my mom, we wouldn't have had anything that year. So I want to pay it forward now that I'm in a better situation."

"Well, I'm glad you're doing better," I offer. "And that you've found someone who can take care of you so you'll never have to experience anything like that again."

"I had another rough patch—not quite as bad—right after I graduated high school. My mom met some guy, got married, and they moved out of state. She told me she'd send some money to help me with my rent, but that never came. She barely had any money for herself. It was hard, getting my feet under me, but I managed. And then I got the job at the bank, met Walt, and I'm about to have my happily-ever-after."

Except, her voice didn't convey that she was happy. She stated it like it was a checklist. Like marrying Walt was just something she had to do to survive. The question I asked her just two days ago sprang to my head again: *Is she sure she should be marrying Walt?*

My thinking was that she wanted the security she'd have by being his wife. She probably likes that more than the man himself.

DECEMBER 15TH
Lexi

❄ ❄ ❄

I've only been home a few minutes after a long day at the bank, but the door swings open again as Walt steps in with a bag of takeout in his hand.

"Oh hey," I say from the kitchen island. I'm sorting through my mail. Electric bill, credit card statement, coupons. After my conversation with Jeff last weekend, I've discovered a newfound gratitude for my ability to pay every bill that comes my way—even if it leaves me pretty tight.

"You ready for dinner?" Walt asks.

"I just need to change." I set the pile of mail on the counter and step into the bedroom, leaving the door ajar so I can talk. "Why don't you pull out some plates for us?"

I open my closet, pull out a sweater, and a pair of sweats from the dresser. Walt wanted to go out tonight, but I convinced him to come over for our date. I figured he'd come casual, but of course he's donning his business suit. The only time I've ever seen him in anything more relaxed was the one time he spent the night. Even then, his pajama set had been ironed before he came.

From the next room, Walt calls out to me, "You don't really have much packed up."

"Well, I'm using the plates every day." Now more comfortable, I open the bedroom door and step back into the other room.

I take a seat on the floor in front of the couch and sift through the puzzle pieces in the box on the coffee table. It's the one I bought at the toy store last weekend. One for me, one for the needy kids.

"You want to sit Indian style?" I offer.

Walt seems distracted. He glances in the bedroom.

"What?" I ask.

"You don't have *anything* packed? Where are your boxes? Totes? Anything?"

"What are you talking about?" I ask.

"We're getting married in *nine days* and moving in together after that." His voice grows in exasperation. It's a side of him I've never seen before. "How long are you going to hold on to this apartment? We need to start packing. Put that puzzle away and let's get started."

Annoyed by the order, I turn back to my puzzle, doing my best to seem unfazed even though my own temper is rising. "Don't worry about it," I tell him. "I have time."

"Nine days, Alexis," he says, as if using my full name is going to make me suddenly comply. "That's not a lot of time. We still need to finalize the plans of the wedding—like the dessert table you've been dragging your feet on—and, oh yeah, there's a major holiday coming the day after we get married!"

Unable to ignore him any longer, I stare at him a moment, chewing on my bottom lip. It's all I can do to keep any venomous words at bay. "I'm very aware of the calendar and the to-do list, Walter."

Two can play at this full-name-game.

"Well then get your head out of the clouds and get the work done," he says. "Get organized. Now, I can help you tonight, but tomorrow this is going to be on you." He turns to the kitchen and starts opening drawers and cabinet doors, inspecting it all. "Let's see here, we can probably pack up some of this Tupperware and things you don't use on regular basis." He pulls out various items stashed below, which makes me spring to my feet to stop him.

"Walt, cut it out." I hold out my hand for him to give me the dishes he's already set on the counter, but he ignores me. "Knock it off, I can do it myself."

He sets the dishes on the counter, reaching down for more.

"Would you just *stop*?" I finally yell.

That catches his attention and he turns to look at me with wild eyes. "I'm trying to help you get your life together. Would you rather we hired movers?"

"No, I don't want strangers touching all of my stuff," she says. "I told you I'd get to it, so just let it be."

"Just let it be like I let the dessert table be? I thought it'd take you two days, tops. Why the hell is it dragging on for almost two weeks?"

My eyes flare with anger. "Listen, I work all day and when I come home I'm tired. Excuse me for trying to find some enjoyment during *the most wonderful time of the year*! Besides, your mother's been in charge of all of the wedding plans so far. I was waiting for her to step in and take over with this, too. Unless she's already finalized it and you're just humoring me?"

Walt rolls his eyes. "Of course she hasn't taken over this. I told you this was yours and I meant it."

"Oh, well, I'm glad that right before the wedding you allow the bride to *finally* have a say in her big day."

"You've had a say this whole time. If you didn't like something, you should've opened your mouth and said so!"

"And deal with the wrath of your mother? No thanks, I've already been subjected to enough judgment from her, thank you very much."

We study each other, both of us too consumed with anger to let the argument go, but also aware enough not to say something we'd regret. Besides, this is an argument that we should've had back when we first started planning the wedding.

"You understand that when you tell me what to do or treat me like a child or *let* me plan the tiniest detail of our wedding, it is incredibly patronizing," I say. "You get that, don't you?"

"You are completely blowing this out of proportion."

"Ah, right. You can't see it from my side, so the problem must be me. Well, until we're married, this is still my apartment and right now I think I want you to leave."

Walt looks at me, a little stunned, likely not sure if I'm serious or not.

"Take your food, get back in your car, and drive back home," I say. "I don't want to talk to you for the rest of the night."

Still, he remains where he is.

Deciding to help him out, I walk over, grab his coat by the door and the bag of food from the counter and hand them both to him. "Come on, I'm not kidding around. Until you're ready to treat me as an equal, I want you to leave me alone."

Slowly, he takes his coat and the food. "I'll call you in the morning."

I open the door for him. "Whatever you want to do. I'll decide if I want to answer, but I need tonight to myself."

He studies me for a few more seconds before conceding to the fact that I'm the one bossing him around now. Surprisingly, he doesn't get defensive like I thought he might. He starts to lean in for a kiss on the cheek, but I back away. A cold move, but I need to draw the line, especially if this is a preview of what our marriage is going to look like.

"I'll call you," he says again before leaving.

When I shut the door, I rest my back against it and take three deep breaths, trying to relax. The tension I'm feeling isn't healthy in the least. Shouldn't I be looking forward to my wedding?

Either way, I need a distraction. Something to get my mind off of Walt, Prudence, and the wedding — even Christmas.

The small tree in the corner by the window is taunting me with its holiday cheer. I step toward it, considering turning off the lights, but something out the window distracts me. Walt is already on the phone as he walks to his car in the parking lot across the street. I look over at my own phone sitting on the coffee table beside the puzzle. It's not ringing, so he's not calling me.

It's probably his mother, who is always looking

for another reason to deem me unworthy of marrying her son.

After Walt's driven away, I reach for my own phone. Sitting in this apartment and stewing is not going to help me relax. I need to get out. No amount of puzzle-solving or book reading will help me unwind.

Before I even realize exactly what I'm doing, I'm calling up Jeff's number on my phone. I hit dial before I have a chance to stop myself, cringing as it rings.

Is it too late to hang up now? Will he call back? What if he's busy? Or working? Or getting tired of me? I should hang up before—

"Hello?"

"Jeff, hi." I make a fist with my hand and slowly bring it against my forehead, feeling stupid for calling him in a moment of weakness. "Are you busy?"

"Just wrapping some of the presents I got last weekend," he says. "It's the only day off I have all week, really."

"Oh, I see. Never mind then. I was just wondering if you wanted to get some coffee or something, but if you're busy—"

"No, it's okay. I can run out for a bit. Where did you want to go? The place on Jackson, near your place? I could meet you there in, say, ten minutes?"

I nod, then realize he can't see that. "Okay. Yeah,

that sounds great."

"Awesome. See you then."

When he hangs up, I smile. Jeff will be able to help me relax.

❈ ❈ ❈

"TO BE HONEST, this meeting has nothing to do with the wedding," I admit as we settle into a pair of comfortable chairs by the window. My steaming mocha latte sits beside me next to Jeff's decaf coffee.

He grins as he lowers himself into his own seat. "I had a hunch, since everything for the wedding is basically taken care of. Less than ten days. Getting nervous?"

"You could say that."

He waits for me to continue, even though it means waiting in silence for an awkward length of time. He's patient and I like that.

"I guess I just needed a break from being…" I pause, searching for the right word before settling on, "fake."

Jeff raises his eyebrows. "You think you're fake?"

"Not all the time." My attention goes to my lap where I fuss with my cuticles.

"While I'm fully aware that I don't know you that well, from what I've seen you're very genuine. You mean what you say. You aren't afraid to be yourself—to explore all of your interests, even while you're navigating everything life's thrown at you. It's inspiring."

I can feel my cheeks flush as they rise with a reluctant smile. "Oh, please."

"I mean it. People like you are good people to have in life. And the more you stick to who you are, the more you're going to draw in similar people. You shouldn't have to be fake—and you're not."

My smile fades. "Not with you, at least."

Jeff pauses with his mug halfway to his mouth. "With Walt?"

I shrug. "To be honest, it's how I've felt this entire engagement. Like I've been putting on a role. Acting like the person I'm *supposed* to be and not the person that I am. Between the formal dinner parties and the appearances at this event or that event and sending a card to this person but calling that other person…" I shake my head. "All for appearances and status. To look good in *someone else's* eyes. People I've only met once. People I've never met. People I don't care to impress." I reach for my drink and take a careful sip. "I'm just tired of it all."

"I can imagine that would be exhausting," he says. "You shouldn't have to pretend to be someone else."

I nod. "I know."

"Then why are you?" He doesn't ask it in an accusatory manner or in a way that makes me defensive. He simply presents it as a new idea. As if the choice were as simple as turning off a light switch.

Still, the simplicity of his question throws me off. "What?"

"Why are you acting like someone you're not?" he asks again.

"Well, it's not really that simple—"

"Sure it is. Be yourself. If Walt and his family don't like it, then now's the time to realize that."

"I can't throw away a whole relationship—one I've promised to make a lifelong commitment to—just because I don't feel comfortable with his way of living."

Jeff stares at me intently. "A lifelong commitment built on a charade is going to make neither of you happy. You shouldn't have to put on an act your whole life. And when you walk down the aisle, that's what you're committing to—your whole life."

Immediately, my thoughts go to my conversation with Tracy Slater last week at that Christmas party. The one where she said that she once married the wrong man. But this is different. Tracy's first husband was abusive. Walt has never laid a finger on me and he never will. He wants to take care of me.

Although, a part of me knows that by insisting on different things, all of which I comply to eventually, he's in effect controlling me little-by-little.

Jeff opens his jacket and pulls a folded piece of

paper from it. "Here, this is for you."

"What is it?" I ask as I take it from him.

He smiles at me. "Just open it."

Slowly, I unfold the paper, my skin prickling with anticipation.

It's a drawing, sketched out on a piece of computer paper. Some of the pencil etching is smeared, but the basic image is still there: me, sitting on the floor of a room that looks strikingly similar to my living room. In the image, I'm working on a puzzle on the coffee table, the end of which has a small stack of books.

"You drew this?"

He nods. "I had a little downtime during my break today."

My eyes grow wide. "You did this on your *break*?"

"Just a little something," he says with a bashful grin. "It's not perfect. I wish I didn't fold it, but I thought you'd like it regardless."

"I love it," I tell him. "Nobody has ever given me a gift like this before."

Jeff waves it off and takes another sip of his coffee, still embarrassed by the praise I'm giving him.

"I'm really glad I met you." My attention is split between studying the drawing and looking into Jeff's eyes. Regardless of which, I know I'm looking right into his soul. His good-natured heart.

"Me too," he says with a smile.

My own smile fades a bit as a thought comes to

me. The reason Jeff and I met is my wedding — which is only next week. After that, what reason will we have to see each other?

DECEMBER 17TH
Jeff

❄ ❄ ❄

The sound of muffled voices from down the hall wakes me. At first I'm disoriented, before I realize that it's the middle of the night. Or rather, early morning. Listening closely, I try to make out what the voices are saying. Quickly, I identify them as Michael and Maddie, which makes sense as I hope there would be no one else in the house at this hour.

"…what's the harm? What difference does a couple hours make?" Maddie asks in a hushed tone.

"Exactly! Whether you take the test now or take it when we wake up, the answer will still be the same!"

"But I'm not going to be able to sleep until I know. And I have a strong feeling this time, Michael."

"You've had a strong feeling the last three times too." A

pause, then, "I'm sorry. I just don't want you to get your hopes up."

"You're not a woman, you don't know. I swear, there's something going on with my body. I just—I need to do this."

Another pause, then, "Okay."

I hear the bathroom door squeak as she closes it.

Silently, I send a prayer up that Michael and Maddie will become parents, and soon. I'm not really the praying type, but I know how much they both want this. And I know how great they'll be at it.

It's almost cruel to witness the quiet heartbreak they endure over and over again as they hope for different outcomes. With each passing month, their demeanor seems to dim a bit more. Especially Maddie. No doubt she feels responsible for not getting pregnant.

That was one thing I wish had been different about my own marriage. That we hadn't waited to try to have kids. Maybe if we had them right away, I'd still have a piece of Alice with me today. Then again, I probably never would've bought the comic shop. Not that that turned out in my favor.

Just as my consciousness is fading again and I drift off to sleep, I hear murmured voices, followed by Maddie's sobs. Even though I can't see them, I imagine Michael comforting her, holding her, leading her back to bed where they can be with each other in private.

This whole journey of theirs has been private. I've only witnessed the last few months of it, but I know they've been trying for a while. Probably closer to a year. It makes me think back to different times they've celebrated friends or family members having babies, all the while wishing there was a celebration for their own child.

My heart aches for my brother and his wife and, even though I just sent one only a few minutes ago, I send up another prayer. Hopefully this time someone's listening.

❄ ❄ ❄

"MR. STONE, DO you have a minute?" Mr. Woodward asks me when I get into work the next morning. "I want an update on our special arrangement."

Lexi. He wants an update on Lexi.

I hang my coat up in the break room and step into his office.

"Shut the door," he says from behind his desk. He has his reading glasses perched on the end of his nose and a paper in front of him.

I close the door and take a seat across from him.

"So, uh, how are things going?" he asks. "The arrangement's working out well?"

I nod. "Yeah, I think so. I've met with Miss Robbins a few times. Showed her some sketches of layouts I came up with, been in touch with the baker already about her decisions. I'll have a more formal contract brought up by the end of the day today."

"Good, good." Mr. Woodward sets the paper down on his desk, along with his glasses. He leans back in his chair and clasps his hands together.

"So we're just about done," I continue. "I know it took me a little bit with this, but I was trying to juggle my other responsibilities here and, you know, I'm still learning how to do this side of the business and everything."

"Of course, yeah," he says. "I'm happy as long as the guests are happy."

"Okay." I nod, but don't dare get up. I can tell there's more he wants to say. My mind races as I think of what that could be. What else could I have done wrong that he'd want to talk to me about in private?

Finally, I build up the courage to ask plainly. "Is there anything else?"

Mr. Woodward sighs heavily, staring at his desk. Finally, he brings his eyes up to me. "Mrs. Connell called."

My heart rate picks up. Lexi is about to become a Connell.

"They're…well, they're a little upset, to be honest."

My mouth goes dry. I try to swallow, but it doesn't help. "With what?"

"They're under the impression that you've been spending a lot of time with the bride. In a way that they don't feel is appropriate for a soon-to-be-married woman to spend with a single guy such as yourself. To be quite frank, she even implied that the two of you might've been seeing each other on a...*personal* basis."

"We're not!" I blurt. How did Mrs. Connell come to that assumption? Did she see us somewhere? Hear gossip? It's a small town, so people talk, but if that's the case, then they know that nothing has ever happened between the two of us. Maybe lingering glances or prolonged smiles, but I barely so much as shook her hand, let alone do anything more.

But still, that doesn't matter. Mr. Woodward is running a business. Mrs. Connell is looking out for her son. I'm the one who will naturally disappear from their lives after the wedding—the one where Lexi will come out as somebody's *wife*.

Everybody must think I'm a creep.

Mr. Woodward puts up his hand to quiet me. "I know. I trust you. And I told her as much. However, you know how Mrs. Connell can be—how *all* of our guests can be." He chuckles to lighten the mood, but it does nothing to soothe my growing fear that I've caused major ripples in many people's lives.

"Have you been spending a lot of time with Miss Robbins?"

"Not a lot," I tell him.

He studies me and the silence is enough pressure to make me cave.

"I think, maybe, there might have been a few lines crossed—or blurred," I admit. "We just got along better than I expected. Maybe we became friendlier than we should've. But nothing inappropriate happened! I guess should've acted in a more professional manner and for that, I'm sorry. I didn't represent the Manor in the way that I should have and I will take all personal responsibility for any repercussions."

Mr. Woodward smirks. "No need to be too hard on yourself, Mr. Stone. You're young. Things happen. She's a pretty girl. A nice girl. But, as you said, you're just about done working with her. So for the time being, why don't you take this as a lesson learned and keep a more professional relationship with Miss Robbins, okay?"

"Yes, sir." My fingers are ice cold and clammy, but I keep them locked together to prevent them from shaking.

"All right, why don't you work on that contract for me? I want to get it submitted before any official orders are made."

After I leave, I head back to the break room. In the pocket of my coat, I pull out my phone and type an apology to Lexi. I don't want her to feel like I wasn't respectful of her relationship with Walt. In hindsight, I'm kicking myself for ever suggesting to her that she *shouldn't* marry him. Maybe that's where all of this is coming from.

With the message typed out, apologizing for any lines crossed, my thumb hovers over the "Send" button, but think better of it. Instead, I hit the backspace again and again until the message is gone.

The only way to fix this is to keep my distance. That means not texting Lexi. She's getting married. I'm not going to mess that up for her.

December 17th
Lexi

❄ ❄ ❄

"Hey, do you think this sweater is okay?" I ask Walt as I get into his car outside my apartment. "I know we usually dress up to go to your parents' but I thought this would be okay too."

He glances over at me from behind the wheel with an unkind look.

"I can run up and change if you want." In reality I don't really want to. I've spent all day dressed up at work, the last thing I want to do on a Friday night is continue to be dressed up in an environment that already puts me on edge.

And Walt's attitude is not setting a good tone for the evening.

With no response, I decide to take my chances with

Prudence's wrath. Before I have a chance to pull on my seatbelt, he whizzes out of the parking lot and toward Main Street.

"What's the matter?" I ask when we get to the light. We usually have a more open relationship where we can talk about things we're annoyed with—usually not each other. Of course, Walt is usually not the one who's angry.

"I heard a rumor that set me off, that's all."

"Oh." My mind churns with ideas about what the rumor could be about that would make him this upset. He doesn't get unhinged easily.

"About you and some guy," he offers.

My heart starts pounding. "What guy?"

"I think that's for you to tell me." He glances over at me. "Is there something you want to tell me?"

I stammer, then notice the light has changed to green. Wordlessly, I point at it and Walt zips through his turn, hitting the brakes behind the line of cars at the Court Street light.

"Well, I'm not really sure what to say because it's obvious you've already made up your mind about the situation before you've even had a chance to hear my side of the story."

He scoffs. "Please, I've had *numerous* people ask me if you and I broke up because you've been looking pretty flirty with this guy. You're not exactly hiding it."

My mind flashes with all of those times I spent

with Jeff—so innocently, but still more time than a betrothed woman should've been spending with a single man.

Actually, no. I'm a grown woman who did not do anything wrong. I'm not about to let anyone—much less my future husband—dictate who I can and can't see. This is a boundary I need to set in this relationship before I commit to a lifetime of this.

"There's nothing to hide, Walter." My body slams backward against the seat as he hits the gas with exaggerated force, braking hard at the intersection with Ellicott Street.

"These damn lights!"

I ignore his attempt at a distraction. "You don't trust me. Do you really think I would sneak around with someone else? Right before our wedding? What kind of person do you think I am?"

"Well, how do you think it makes me feel?" he asks, stabbing his finger into his chest. He's over-gesturing to further drive home the point that he's angry.

Note taken, Walt. I've already picked up on that.

"It's embarrassing for you to be gallivanting all over town when you're going to be my wife in less than a week!"

I reel my head back and study him, surprised at the overt expressions of control he's spewing. "Whether I'm someone's *wife* or not, I have a right to spend time with whomever I want. If you have a problem with who I'm hanging out with, *talk* to me like a rational person and maybe I'll consider backing off. But you need to respect me and my choices enough if I decide not to listen to your concerns. That's how marriages work, Walter. *Compromise*."

"Like you would know anything about—" He catches himself before he finishes what would be a death sentence to our whole relationship. Still, I got the gist of what he intended.

Grabbing on to the bar above my head as he makes the turn toward the traffic circle, I keep my eyes on him as best I can.

"Do you even want to marry me?" I ask, trying not to let his reckless driving get to me.

He keeps his eyes on the road as he passes the exit for South Main Street and continues around the circle back toward Main. I wonder where he's going, but don't voice it.

"Of course I do," he says with absolutely no enthusiasm.

"Well, sometimes it's hard for me to feel that because all you do is treat me like a child. Like I can be controlled. I'm not a *dog*, Walter, you can't dictate every aspect of my life."

His jaw clenches, but he doesn't say anything as he continues back down Main Street. This time, he hits every green light until we're turning onto Jackson Street. Back to my apartment.

"What are we doing?" I finally ask.

Abruptly, he pulls off to the side and stops the car. "I'm dropping you off. I'll go to my parents' alone."

I watch him, surprised by this sudden turn of events. The first thing I learned about Walt and his family is that they are very much about keeping appearances. Arriving to dinner without me would send a big message to his parents. One that would only further give credence to Prudence's dislike of our impending marriage.

"Fine." I unbuckle and reach for the door handle. "I need time to think by myself too."

I step out and shut the door, expecting him to wait for me to cross the street before he leaves. This time, however, he doesn't.

❄ ❄ ❄

MONDAY, DECEMBER 20TH

"TEN, TWENTY, THIRTY, forty, *fifty*—one, two, three, four, *fifty-five*," I say robotically as I dish out the money to the next member at work. "You're all set. Is there anything else I can get for you?"

"No thanks," the old woman tells me with a smile. She tucks her cash in her purse, then pulls out her gloves. Tossing her purse over her shoulder, she tells me, "Merry Christmas," before heading toward the door.

My mind is elsewhere as I assist the next member—someone who seems to just be starting to do their own banking. They walk with a certain level of hesitance, unsure of their moves exactly, but going through the motions just as everyone else is.

All of these notices happen without me really having to try too hard because my thoughts are mostly wrapped up in Walt. We didn't talk for most of the weekend. Last night he called to apologize for his accusations, telling me that I was right and he needs to trust me more.

Reluctantly, I found myself apologizing for the part I played in creating any rumors. We both agreed that it was probably pre-wedding jitters that caused our argument and we made arrangements to have dinner tonight. It'll be a nice way to reconnect, but I can't help but wonder how much my heart is in it. The worst part of this weekend was the realization that I only missed Walt a little bit. The homerun hit was the nagging urge to reach out to Jeff to help me pick up the pieces after Friday's argument.

I resisted the thoughts of both men as best I could.

"Good morning, how are—oh."

The next member to come through my line is none other than Jeff himself. My cheeks flush with the childish wonder if he could read my thoughts.

"Hey," he says, his tone somber. He sets a wad of cash and a deposit slip in front of me. "I'm just putting this in my account."

I take his money and count it out, making sure it matches what's written on the deposit slip. Then I turn to my computer and type in the adjustments. "Sorry for not getting back that contract to you." Jeff had emailed me a contract on Friday that I needed to sign off on before he could include it in the bill for the wedding. It was still sitting in my inbox.

He waves it off. "No rush. As long as it's before the date of the event—uh, I mean, the wedding."

We smile awkwardly at each other.

"It's been a bit of a rough weekend," I admit. I hit enter and a receipt prints. "All I wanted to do was watch movies and eat too much. Probably just...girl stuff." I try to downplay it by using the one thing I know would make any guy uncomfortable: *girl stuff*.

"Actually, I think I should be the one apologizing."

I furrow my brow as I stick his deposit slip in the right slot to be collected later. I tear off his receipt from the printer and hand it to him. "Apologizing for what?"

"I didn't mean to cross any lines in our professional relationship," he says. "You were a client and I should've kept it as such. I'm sorry."

This apology is likely the work of the Connells. They probably complained to the Manor, which is something they would do in order to maintain their status as a powerful force in the community.

"You did nothing wrong," I assure him. "You were an acquaintance who became a friend. I told you, I don't have too many of those."

He smiled shyly and looked down as he folded the receipt again and again. Eventually, he met my eyes again. "Well, it wasn't hard…"

With a sigh, I continue speaking before he can. "I do think it's probably better if you and I…take a break from hanging out for a while."

Inside, I'm kicking myself for caving to the pressure like this. All weekend I've been debating what I should do about Jeff. The simple fact is that while a man isn't a good husband if he controls his wife, a woman isn't a good wife if she constantly ignores her husband's feelings. As much as I want Walt to be a good husband to me, I want to be a good wife to him.

Compromise.

Jeff's smile quickly disintegrates. "Right. That makes sense."

"It's just that the wedding is in four days and there's a lot to do—like getting that contract back to you, among other things. I just think it's best if I focus on that for now. You understand, right?"

"Of course, yeah. You're getting married!" He feigns excitement and I can't help but feel like I hurt him. "You should be focused on that."

"I do appreciate all of your help," I offer.

"Just doing my job," he says. "Well, since I won't

be seeing you, good luck with the wedding. And merry Christmas."

"Merry Christmas," I reply.

He turns and I watch as he walks out the door, a part of me wishing things could be different.

DECEMBER 23RD
Jeff

* * *

"Dinner was delicious, honey," Michael tells Maddie after we've finished eating. She's been noticeably down all week. The reason for which has been a closely guarded secret, although they don't know that I overheard them the other night.

She offers a half smile and gathers all the dirty plates. "Thanks, sweetheart." All the life has been drained from her voice.

"Leave those, Mads," Michael says when she reaches the sink. "Jeff and I will get them. Why don't you go up and run a bath or relax in front of the TV or something?"

She doesn't argue, but walks up behind her husband and rubs his shoulders. "Thanks. I could use a break."

He squeezes her hand and brings it to his mouth to

kiss it. "No problem. Just relax."

When I'm sure she's out of earshot, I rise and gather the remaining dishes on the table. "Ordinarily I'd complain about being volunteered for extra work, but I agree that she needs a break."

Michael turns on the water and holds his fingers under it to test the temperature. "She's been having a rough time lately. She'll get through it."

"Of course, yeah." I pull out some Tupperware and distribute the leftovers into the containers before setting the used cooking dishes beside the sink for Michael to wash.

"So what's been your deal?"

My head snaps over in his direction, but Michael's focus is on filling the sink. "What do you mean?"

"You've been very mopey lately too," he says. "Geez, it's Christmastime and this place has the atmosphere of a funeral. Where's the holiday spirit?"

I set the leftover containers in the fridge. "Just haven't been feeling it lately, I guess."

"Come on," Michael pushes. "Level with me. What's up?"

With a sigh, I decide there's no harm divulging what's been keeping me down the past few days. After all, I'm very aware of the problems Michael and Maddie are facing, which is usually contained within the confines of a marriage. By comparison, my problems aren't so bad.

"Well, you know how Mr. Woodward gave me that opportunity to do some planning work for a wedding?"

"The one you didn't want to do but we talked you into doing it anyway? Yeah, I remember. What about it?"

Rolling my eyes, I grab a towel and start drying the dishes Michael has set on the counter. "I started meeting with the bride — Lexi — and she ended up not being so bad."

"See? What did we tell you?"

"I could do without the 'I told you so.'"

"Sorry. So what's the problem? Did she not like what you came up with?"

"No, that's not it." I pile the dinner plates on top of each other in the cabinet. "She and I became friends. Started hanging out a little outside of the Manor. It was completely innocent, but her boyfriend didn't like it so we both agreed that we needed to stop hanging out."

Michael shrugs. "I could see that. I mean, the whole reason you met her was because she's getting married."

"Right." I work at drying a handful of silverware and drop them in the drawer.

"But you miss her," he says, probably sensing that there's more to the story. We have a knack for knowing what the other's thinking. It's both annoying and kind of cool.

"Yeah, I do. And I know that she's getting married tomorrow, but I'm not convinced that she really loves him. I think she just likes the idea of being married so that she'll always have someone to catch her when she falls. She's even admitted that she enjoys spending time with me. And she's called me a few times to hang out because of an argument she's been having with her boyfriend. And I know, it could just be nerves before the wedding, but I can't help but feel like I'm losing someone really special. Something I haven't had since Alice."

He's quiet, which only adds to my anxiety as I wait for his response. This is the perfect opportunity for him to make fun of me. Tell me that I'm crazy for pining after a woman who is going to be someone's wife in twenty-four hours. That I should just move on before I'm too invested.

Too late. I'm in deeper than I thought. It hit me the moment Lexi told me we needed to stop hanging out.

"I just really miss her," I say in his silence. "And I know it's stupid. She's not mine—she never was. But I just wish things were different. I'll get over it. This is probably just a crush anyway. And it's a good sign that I'm heading in the right direction, right? I mean, it's been five years since Alice and Lexi's the first girl I could see myself having a future with. There will be others."

Still, Michael is quiet. He finishes up washing

what dishes are left in the sink, then turns off the water and grabs a towel to dry his hands. "Have I ever told you the story of when Maddie and I first started dating?"

"You guys were in college together," I say. "I just figured you gave her some lame pick-up line and she took pity on you."

He smirks. "Funny, but no. She was the one I saw all over campus, involved in all these clubs and other activities. School newspaper, debate team, yoga classes, volleyball, RA, you name it, she probably did it in those four years. And, of course, you know I was the one who was very interested in one particular *extra curricular*."

Drinking. My brother was a huge drinker in college. Until he started dating Maddie, that is. Surprisingly, his senior year was his driest one ever.

"Yes, I'm aware."

"My point is, I didn't think I stood a chance with her. But I took a chance and asked her out. Turns out, she saw me running around the park and liked what she saw." He holds out his hands and smirks again. "And, I mean, who could blame her?"

I roll my eyes. "There's one big difference between your story and mine: Maddie wasn't engaged to someone else."

"True, but if I hadn't asked her out, do you think I'd be married to her now?" He lets the question hang there before adding, "Give it a shot. Tell this girl how you feel. Lexi, right? Maybe she's thinking the same thing too but feels stuck. She doesn't want to say anything because she doesn't want to admit it to herself that she likes you — God only knows why."

I swat the towel at him.

"I'm just saying, she has more to lose than you do. So tell her how you feel and let her make the final decision. If she decides to leave her boyfriend — like you suspect she might be thinking already — then it's her decision. Don't pressure her, just tell her where you stand. If not, she'll always be the one who got away. By Christmas morning, it'll be too late."

His words hit me. They terrify me, actually. I haven't put myself out there since Alice, but he's right. I'm not going to have anyone else until I put myself out there again.

And soon. The countdown is on to Lexi's wedding. I can't let her walk down that aisle without telling her how I feel.

If there's one thing I've realized in the last two days, it's that I'm falling in love with Alexis Robbins.

DECEMBER 24TH
Lexi

❄ ❄ ❄

*I*t's my wedding day.

And yet, I am not the least bit excited. Sure, the temperature has dropped for the first time this season and I know the Manor will look beautiful if it does end up snowing like they say it might, but none of it feels like *mine*. I'll be the center of attention, sure, but more so because I'm the nameless bride. Not because I'm marrying the love of my life and celebrating that love.

I lay in bed, watching a couple flurries float through the air. Killing time until I need to get up and take a shower.

Most girls have a whole entourage of people to help them get ready for their wedding. I'll have some of the female staff at the Manor helping me. And I'm sure

Prudence will pop in now and then. Certainly not the grand fanfare I thought I would have on my wedding day when I was a little girl. The numerous disappointments make me want to stay here in bed and forget the world for the day.

All of this hesitation stems from the argument Walt and I had last weekend, which stemmed from the serious question Jeff asked me before: should I really be marrying Walt?

Getting married is a big decision and I want to make sure I'm making the right one. I thought I'd know for sure on the morning of my wedding, but I don't and that scares me. Do all brides feel the same way right before they walk down the aisle? Or do they say their vows with absolute certainty that the man in front of them is the one that's right for them? How do we ever really know for sure?

Rolling over, I reach for the sketch Jeff made me and can't help but smile. This small gesture of his brings more happiness into my life than the thought of spending my whole day at this wedding.

Again, that scares me. How did a stranger swoop into my life so quickly and make such an impact? And is it a genuine impact or just something that I'm clinging to in the fear that my relationship with Walt has serious cracks?

And it does have cracks. Last weekend proved that. It was the first time in a while that I stood up for myself and pointed out the way he was treating me.

And although he apologized over the phone, the last few days have shown that that apology was hollow.

In the days leading up to today's big event, Walt has continued to treat me as an afterthought or leave me out of decisions completely. Whether that be an innocent act or not, it tells a lot: he cares more about the wedding and the status he's about to gain than he does me.

Not that he doesn't care about me. He does. Just not in the way a husband should.

That thought, in all of its enormous simplicity, makes me sit up straight in bed. I love Walt in the sense that I care for his wellbeing and wish him happiness for his life. But I don't love him as a wife. And if I don't love him as a wife, then I can't go through with the wedding today. As much as I know it'll crush him, I just can't go through with it.

Not when there's someone else bringing a smile to my face.

Holding Jeff's sketch close to my chest, I look up to the ceiling and take a deep breath, building the courage to make the difficult phone call.

Walt answers on the first ring and his voice is hesitant. "Hey Lexi, what's up?"

I suck in my lips, feeling my throat constricting with emotion. "Do you think you could come over here? Like, now?"

Voices sound on the other end, likely the entourage that has already showed up for Walt's preparation for the wedding. It's further proof that we come from different worlds and is another reminder that I'm making the right choice. As far as his family's concerned, this wedding could be happening with any girl.

"I'm kind of in the middle of something right now," he says. "Besides, it's bad luck for the bride and groom to see each other before the wedding." He forces a laugh. "I'm not even sure we should be talking on the phone. Isn't that against the rules too?"

"Well, that's the thing…" I pause to take in another breath to build up my courage further. "We need to talk about…a lot, actually. Things we've been putting off."

He doesn't answer at first, his silence telling me that he's putting it all together. "We couldn't have had this conversation before?"

Squeezing my eyes shut, I say, "Honestly, I think that's what we were trying to do last weekend when we fought. I don't think this is the right choice, Walt."

He sighs. "But…the wedding. And my parents. And they've already paid for everything."

My knee-jerk reaction is to tell him that this is more important than money, but I don't want him to be mad at me. Not anymore than he likely already is. "I'm sorry. But it's better now than after the wedding. I—I don't think there should be a wedding at all."

He's quiet again, and I can picture him nodding.

"I thought you might say that."

"It's not that I don't care about you," I say quickly. "I do, but I don't think I'm the person who is going to be a good wife to you. I'm sorry."

He doesn't say anything. In the background, I can hear the hum of voices laughing, talking, beginning to celebrate.

"Are you mad?" I ask quietly.

Another pause, then, "No. Disappointed, yes. But if I'm being honest, I think we both realized this wasn't going to work a while ago. I just didn't want to upset anyone."

At his words, I feel as though a weight has been lifted from my shoulders. "I do care about you."

"I know. And I love you, but if you're not going to be happy with me then I don't think we should get married. And don't worry about my parents. I'll take care of it."

"Are you sure? Maybe we can work out a payment plan so I can pay them back for everything they're going to miss out on."

He chuckles softly, trying to lighten the mood. "I'm sure they'd take you up on that, but don't worry about it. I'll take care of it. Go and live your life. I hope you have a good one—and that you find someone who's good to you."

Jeff's sketch falls down into my lap, as if on cue. "Thank you. I wish you well too. Maybe after a while we can even be friends."

"Maybe." The tone of his voice tells me that that's unlikely. "Goodbye Lexi."

"Bye Walt."

IT TOOK ME all afternoon—and several failed phone calls—but I finally talked myself into going to the Manor. The snow has started to pick up and it takes me a minute to remember how to drive in it, but now I'm well on my way to LeRoy to see Jeff.

The last thing I wanted to do was run into Walt—or his family—when I decide to take a leap and try things out with Jeff. Or see if he wants to. But in the end I decided that today, being Christmas Eve, I was going to take chances and be unafraid of falling on my face.

Who knows? Maybe in one day I'd lose both Walt and Jeff. Even if Jeff does turn me down, I know now that I'll be happier not marrying Walt. Prudence and Walter the Second are just going to have to deal. Hopefully Walt makes good on his promise that he'd take care of them.

The closer I get to LeRoy, the worse the snow gets. The first snowfall of the year is really making an entrance. Despite the thickening whiteness, I spot a car come up in the opposite lane, driving in the opposite direction. Being the only thing I can see through the snow, I focus on it so I don't swerve out of my lane and hit it or go off the road.

As it careens closer, it begins to look familiar and my eyes search for the driver. In a split second, I catch a fraction of a view of Jeff behind the wheel. He notices me too and I immediately take my foot off the gas, looking for a place to pull over.

Emery Park is just up on the left and I pull into the gravel parking lot, half of me hoping that I don't get stuck on my way out and the other half hoping that Jeff actually turns around and joins me. What I have to say can't wait to follow him home — or be said over the phone. I already called off a wedding over the phone, I wasn't about to make a second social crime in one day.

Luckily, Jeff's car pulls into the parking lot shortly after me. He doesn't even find a proper parking spot like I did, but pulls up behind me and puts the car in park. There's no one else here so it doesn't matter.

I get out into the snow, bracing myself against the cold but not feeling it much because of the burning in my stomach.

"I heard you called off the wedding," he says, coming around his car. He stops a few feet away from me.

"I did."

"Why?"

"Because I realized that I have feelings for someone else."

He hesitates.

"You," I offer.

"Me?" His mouth curls up in a smile.

"All my life I've been searching for someone like you," I say. "Someone who sees me. Who wants what's best for me. Who's my best friend. *And* someone who will take care of me. I thought I had too much on my wish list, so I settled for someone who only did some of those things. Until you came into my life and showed me that I wasn't asking for too much at all. I was asking for exactly what I need."

The snow clings to both of us, sticking to our hair, our jackets, our cars. But neither of us pay it much notice. We're both too captivated by each other's eyes.

"And now I know that's you," I continue. "I love you, Jeff. And I know we still have a lot to learn about each other, but I can feel it in my soul that you're the one for me. And I don't want anyone else."

Jeff closes the distance between us and embraces me. "I've been hoping you'd feel the same. Lexi, I love you. I never thought I'd tell another woman that in my life. After my wife passed away and my business went under, I thought I had exhausted all of my opportunities. But you helped me see that there are so many opportunities still waiting for me to explore. You've given me a second chance at life and I can't wait to take it head-on with you."

I smile and reach up to cup his face between my

gloved hands. "Then let's stop talking and get started."

He leans down and we kiss, losing ourselves in the winter wonderland that has suddenly sprung up around us in a matter of hours. Despite standing in the frigid air, I feel warm, content, and safe in Jeff's arms.

Most of all, I feel excited for the future. The man I love doesn't need to be my husband before we can start the rest of our lives. It starts the moment we give in to what our heart desires.

DECEMBER 24TH
Jeff

❄ ❄ ❄

Lexi finishes tidying up the kitchen in the back while I handle the two customers in the shop. Steph and Carson, two out-of-towners who picked Batavia to spend the holidays for its small town charm.

Carson sets down a book on the counter beside the plate of Christmas cookies Steph bought from us.

"All set?" I ask.

"I think so," Carson says. "Are we your last customers?"

"Last ones for the day," I tell him as I punch their items into the register. "We're closing up for Christmas as soon as you guys leave."

"Oh, then we'd better hurry," Steph says. "We

weren't sure you'd be open today."

"Neither did we." I take her cash and add it to the drawer, counting out the change. "But Lexi wanted to get the rest of the dishes cleaned up and I figured we might as well put the 'Open' sign up and see who wanders in."

"I'm glad you did," Carson says. "You have a great shop. Books and baked goods, count me in."

I laugh. "Merging both of our interests." I hand them their bag.

"Have a nice day and merry Christmas!" Steph calls as they turn to the door.

"Thanks again!" Carson offers.

I wave and watch them step out onto the street. Crossing the shop to the door, I lock it and inspect the street. It's been snowing a bit, but the sidewalk still seems clear. I decide I shouldn't have to shovel it again until at least tomorrow.

Lexi comes out from the back, drying her hands in a towel. "Are you all set?" "Just need to lock up the drawer." I take it from the register and step into the back, where I deposit the cash drawer in the safe. "We had quite a few people stop in today. I'm surprised."

"Last minute shoppers who want to support local businesses," she says. "It's what keeps us afloat."

Last spring, Lexi and I opened our shop, Books and Bakes. Lexi has a full display of delicious treats available—although the bulk of that revenue comes from special orders and catering—and the rest of the shop is lined with books for purchase. Everything from the classics and comics to romance and mysteries. There is plush seating and soft instrumental music playing, creating a warm and cozy atmosphere. Best of all, it's right downstairs from our apartment.

"Ready to go?" Lexi asks once she's donned her hat and coat.

I finish buttoning up mine and then open the door for her. "Do you want to drive or walk?"

"Let's walk," she says.

After I've locked up, I offer my arm and she hooks hers through it. Together, we head toward Main Street on our way to Michael and Maddie's house for a Christmas Eve dinner with them and their daughter, Ruby.

Two days after Christmas last year, they met with fertility specialists to figure out why they weren't having success with trying to have a baby. Long story short, her doctor ordered a blood test and determined that she was already pregnant. The home test she took prior to that visit had been wrong.

"You know what today is?" Lexi asks when we turn onto Main Street.

"Christmas Eve."

"Which means it's technically our one-year anniversary."

I look down at her and smile. "I guess it is. You'll

never figure out what I got you."

"I just assumed you'd forgotten, since it's overshadowed by Christmas."

"I'd never forget the most important day of my life."

Soon to be the second most important day. The anniversary gift I got her is an engagement ring.

A chance moment. A snow storm. And the gift of a new beginning.

Tristan is ready to party and ring in the New Year by kissing his soon-to-be girlfriend, Julie. The only bad note in his rocking night is the ongoing snow storm. Outside his apartment, he's almost hit by a swerving car! Behind the wheel is Grace, the most beautiful woman with haunting green eyes. She's on her own mission to get home to her grandfather.

In a selfless act reminiscent of the age of knights and chivalry, Tristan vows to get her home…never realizing they are both on a date with destiny and their lives will be forever changed by the SNOW AFTER CHRISTMAS…

More by the Author

To find more books by the author, visit
DavidNethBooks.com/Books

* * *

Subscribe to his newsletter to be the first to know of new
releases and special deals!
DavidNethBooks.com/Newsletter

* * *

If you enjoyed the book, please consider leaving a review
on Goodreads or the retailer you bought it from. Reviews
help potential readers determine whether they'll enjoy a
book, so any comments on what you thought of the story
would be very helpful!

ABOUT THE AUTHOR

D. Allen is the author of the sweet small town romance series, Montana Beach and Small Town Christmas.

Also writes fantasy and superhero fiction as David Neth.

www.DavidNethBooks.com
www.facebook.com/DavidNethBooks

www.ingramcontent.com/pod-product-compliance
Lightning Source LLC
Chambersburg PA
CBHW030903200726
48289CB00003B/874